Black Arts & Bones

by

Sara Bourgeois

11

Chapter One

A loud bang sent me scrambling down the stairs. I'd gone up to the bedroom to change into a dress and put on makeup. Laney was in her playpen in the living room, but she was asleep. So, I figured it was fine leaving her undisturbed to finish her nap.

Naturally, the thud made my blood turn to ice water. Meri was in the living room with Laney, but I still shot down the steps so fast that I missed the last two and fell on my knees.

That was going to leave a bruise.

If all that noise hadn't brought Thorn in from outside, I didn't know what would. It didn't wake Laney either.

I, on the other hand, got to witness the full horror of what was unfolding at my fireplace. The thump was the sound of the jar containing Zane's soul hitting the stone hearth. Fortunately, it hadn't shattered, but Samara's spirit stood over it. She appeared to be contemplating her next move.

"What are you doing?" I hissed.

While the sound of the jar hitting the floor hadn't woken Laney, my distressed outcry to the ghost before me did. She sat up, rubbed her eyes, and pleaded, "mama."

I rushed over to the playpen and scooped her into my arms. "Mama's here," I said and kissed her forehead.

It was just babble, and I knew she really didn't know what the word meant, but it pulled at my heartstrings, nonetheless.

I hoped that Samara's spirit would just vanish. It wasn't as if she hung around my house knocking stuff off shelves. In fact, that was the first I'd seen of her since shortly after her death. I'd never expected to see her again.

So, of course she was there.

Trying to set Zane's awful ghost free?

What?

It was supposed to be Thorn's and my first date night since Laney was born, and right on cue, the supernatural began its shenanigans. I was already nervous about leaving her with my parents while we went out on the town.

"What are you doing?" I asked again when Samara didn't answer.

3

She looked up at me and looked back down at the jar. Instead of addressing me, Samara tried to kick the jar. That was followed by her trying to stomp on it. Neither attempt had much effect, and when she stooped down to pick it up, her ghostly hand went right through it.

"You don't have enough energy to do anything more than just knock it off the shelf, apparently," I said. "You're not going to be able to smash it because you can't draw any more energy from this house." That was at least one thing Hangman's House had going for it. The house could also provide me with any money I needed or food I desired, but that wasn't relevant to the current situation.

Samara looked up and me and scowled. "I want… I want…"

She went quiet for a second.

"You want what?" I asked. "Tell me. Maybe I can help you."

"I want my life back," she said with a heaving sigh. "I don't want to be dead. I miss my house. I miss baking."

Her words stabbed me right through the heart. Samara was so sad, but that wasn't uncommon. People were frequently sad when they died before their time. It's the reason things that reminded them of life were so attractive.

"Taking revenge on Zane won't bring you back," I said and stroked Laney's soft curls. She was starting to wiggle in my arms, and I wanted to get rid of Samara before I put her down again.

"I don't want revenge," Samara said. "I want him to put me back."

Oh.

"No," I said so loud that Laney jumped a little in my arms. "Sorry, baby," I said and kissed her forehead. It kept her from bursting into tears. "Mommy's just got to take care of this ghost, and then we'll get you some pears."

"Pears?" Samara's spirit looked at me with heightened interest.

"They're baby pears," I said. "Mashed all to high heck. Besides, you can't eat."

That was a stupid thing to say. I sighed as Samara's face became a mask of fury.

Fortunately, that was the end of it. She poofed out the way I imagined she'd poofed in. I would be infinitely happier when we fixed good magic and I could redo the protection spells and sigils around Hangman's House.

"Well, that was fun," I said to Laney.

She squeezed my cheeks and giggled.

"Come on, cat," I said over my shoulder to Meri. "Pears for the princess and bacon for you. Let's get you dinner before Thorn and I leave."

He was seated on the coffee table licking his paw and then washing his ears. Fat lot of help he'd been. Not that it was his fault.

Thorn arrived home from work a half an hour late. In fact, he showed up at the exact time my parents arrived to watch Laney.

"I have to shower," he said as he took his hat off and hung it over the door.

"You can't," I said. "We have a reservation."

Just then, my mom pinched her nose and scrunched up her face. "Let him take a shower," Mom said as she waved her hand in front of her face.

Dad had already scooped up Laney, and they were headed out to the back yard to look for bugs. It was too late in the year for fireflies, but they could always get into something. He was teaching her to love the creepy-crawly things instead of fear them.

"What's wrong?" I started to ask, but as soon as I was closer to Thorn, I could smell him. "Oh, my gosh, you smell like hogs," I said and covered my nose.

"Yep," he said with a shrug. "Farmer's fence broke and the hogs were blocking traffic on the highway. I got called in to help round them up and wrangle them home."

"Go," I said. "Shower, and don't hurry."

"I'll be squeaking clean in a jiffy," Thorn said as he rushed up the stairs.

"No, really. Take your time," I said with a laugh. "You want tea, Mom?"

"Sure," she said. "You're going to miss your reservation, though. Will you guys have to eat at another restaurant? I know you were looking forward to trying that new steakhouse in the city."

"No, we won't miss it. I always tell Thorn the reservation is for half an hour earlier than it really is. He's super punctual at home, but when it comes to work... he frequently has to deal with issues that don't care about his schedule. I find that if I tell him that he needs to be here a half an hour before he really does, he tends to make it when I need him," I said.

"Good thinking," Mom said.

I made some tea, and we chatted for a while. One cup later, Thorn came downstairs, and I went out to the living room to meet him.

"Wow," I said when I saw him.

He was dressed in a white button-down shirt, but he'd rolled it up to the exact place that showed off his biceps. His black slacks were fitted just right so that they hugged his butt.

"Do I look bad?" he asked and looked down at his attire. "I know the sleave thing is kind of dumb, but it's what's in fashion. I don't know what I was thinking."

He quickly unrolled them and buttoned the cuff. Interestingly enough, the sleeves still accentuated his biceps. "We should go," I said.

"Right, the reservation," Thorn said. "Are your parents all set?"

"We are good. We'll call you if we need anything," Mom said from the dining room doorway.

I'd told her about Samara's ghost making an appearance just before she'd arrived, and Mom had waved it off. She said it was nothing she and my dad couldn't handle.

I walked quickly out to the car and almost dove in before Thorn had a chance to open the door for me. "Sorry we're going to be late," he said just before shutting the passenger door.

What he didn't know was that we weren't going to be late. We just needed to get out of there before I dragged him upstairs to make Laney a little brother or sister. Dang, Thorn looked good, and he smelled even better.

It hit me like a truck when he got in behind the wheel. "You okay?" he asked.

"I'm doing great," I barely squeaked out. "You just look really good, good enough to devour."

"I'd say the same about you, but I don't think the words would do justice," he said and squeezed my knee.

"You'd better pull out of the driveway now, or we're going back inside," I said with a chuckle.

He thought about it for a minute, and then reversed out of the driveway into the street. "As much as I'd love to spend some quality time at home with you, I promised you a night out on the town. So, away we go," Thorn said.

It was a quiet drive into the city. Thorn and I held hands and listened to the car's stereo. Laney wasn't a loud baby by any stretch of the imagination, but even quiet babies are noisy compared to two adults on a car ride. It was like the earth opened up and swallowed all of the sound. The ride was peaceful in a way I didn't even know I'd missed.

"I feel guilty," Thorn said as we pulled into the parking lot at the restaurant.

"Why?" I asked.

"Because the ride here was so peaceful and calm, and I feel bad for thinking it," Thorn said.

"Our lives have been hectic," I replied. "And you've had the added stress of being back at work. I have Reggie and Katherine running the shop for me. Basically, I pop in when I feel like it."

"Yes, but I'm a hundred percent sure that being a full-time mom is more work than being town sheriff," Thorn said. "You never get a day off. At least when I go to work, all I have to worry about is my work."

"I guess I'll just let you keep thinking that," I said. "But as far as feeling guilty because we've had a few calm minutes to ourselves, don't."

Thorn came around and got my door before helping me out of the car. We walked inside the restaurant hand in hand.

I tried not to worry about Laney. Each time I did, I'd get a pang of guilt for being away from her. When that happened, I'd look over at Thorn and study the rough stubble peppering his square jaw.

We had to focus on our marriage too. It was the only way we could be good parents for the long haul.

The host was at the station and seated us right away. I was blown away with the restaurant. It was dim inside with lights that resembled candlelight. The dining area was in a sunken section in the middle of the building. Waitstaff dressed in crisp white shirts and starched black slacks scurried around delivering white plates of perfectly cooked meat that looked more like works of art than meals. Others busied themselves pouring wine or clearing dishes.

We were seated at a booth along the wall to the left. It was cozy without feeling overcrowded. Dinner was delicious but uneventful. Thorn ordered a massive ribeye and I had filet. We mostly made small talk, but eventually the conversation turned to Laney. We discussed her first five months and what we thought it would be like until she turned one.

As Thorn paid the check, my phone rang. My heart jumped into my throat when I saw it was my mother.

"Mom, is Laney okay?" I asked before she could get a word out.

"Is she okay?" Thorn asked.

We were already scooting out of the booth.

"She's fine, honey," Mom said.

"She's okay," I said to Thorn. "Well, then what is it? Is Dad okay? It's not Lilith, is it?"

"It's nothing like that, Kinsley. I hate to bother you, but I think you need to come home," Mom said.

"If everyone is okay, then what's up?"

By that time, Thorn and I were out in the parking lot. We shuffled quickly to the car. He opened the door for me, and I got in. When he got behind the wheel, I fumbled to put my seatbelt on. Eventually, Thorn reached over and helped me click it into place.

"It's going to be too hard to explain over the phone," Mom said. "Laney is fine, but please come home. Your father and I will make it up to you with another date night."

"Okay, Mom. We'll be there as soon as we can," I said and we disconnected.

"What's going on?" Thorn asked as he pulled out of the restaurant's parking lot.

"Laney is fine," I said. "Mom said it was too complicated to explain over the phone but we need to come home."

Thorn and I were silent again on the drive home, and this time the stereo was off. We tried listening to it, but the music made my anxiety worse. Thorn held my hand, and I must have practically squeezed it off.

I knew my mom had said that Laney was fine, but I was terrified something had happened to her and my mother just didn't want to tell me over the phone. Dread crept from my stomach up into my throat the entire excruciating ride home.

By the time we turned onto our street, I felt like my skin was on fire and crawling with ants. It was amazing I didn't jump out of the car while it was still rolling.

The thing that stopped me was the woman sitting on our front steps. I'd seen her around town, but I didn't know her.

She was sitting there with her head on her knees and her arms wrapped around her legs. When she looked up, I could tell she'd been bawling.

There were also ugly purple circles under her eyes like the poor woman hadn't slept in years. Even at the worst of my insomnia, I never looked that bad.

"Should I get my gun?" Thorn asked as he turned the car off.

"I think if she was dangerous, my parents wouldn't let her just sit out on the porch. They probably would have called your deputies," I said. "Let's just go talk to her."

As I was getting out of the car, my mom peeked out the window and pointed at the woman. She gave me a thumbs-up, and I wasn't sure what that was supposed to mean other than that the woman probably wasn't dangerous.

"Hello," I said, and I could feel Thorn behind me. He was so close, I swear I felt his breath on the back of my neck. I elbowed him gently, and he took the hint.

The woman was standing at that point, she came down the last few steps. "You have to help me," she sobbed.

"Well, let's slow it down a bit. I'm Kinsley. What's your name?" I asked.

"I'm sorry," she said and wiped her eyes with the heels of her palms. "I'm Nora Kent."

"It's nice to meet you, Nora," I said. "What do you need help with?"

"I talked to your dad," she said. "He said it was okay for me to wait. He said he would help me if you couldn't or wouldn't."

"I'm sure he would," I said gently. "But tell me what you need?"

"Should I call in one of my deputies?" Thorn asked.

"Oh, you're the sheriff," Nora said before turning back to me. "I almost forgot you were married to the sheriff. No, nothing for the police."

Her eyes shot back and forth between me and Thorn. I realized whatever she wanted my help with, she didn't want to ask in front of Thorn.

"Sweetie, why don't you go in the house and check on Laney," I said to Thorn.

"I think I should stay out here," he said and crossed his arms.

"Thorn, go check on the baby," I rolled my eyes. "I'll be in soon."

"Okay," he said and put his hand up in front of his chest in mock surrender. "Just holler if you need me."

"I need you to come with me," Nora said as Thorn went inside.

"Where?" I asked. "Please tell me what's going on. You're starting to make me nervous."

"I'm sorry," Nora said and then bit her bottom lip. She was about to start crying again. "I've been having a rough week, and I haven't slept in… I don't know how long."

"I can see that," I said. "No offense."

"None taken," she said. "I know I look terrible. It's just that… there's something in my house."

"Something? Like what?"

"Like a ghost or something," she said.

I wasn't quite sure what to say. I didn't really know Nora, but one thing I did know was that she wasn't a witch. I'd need to tread carefully talking about the paranormal if she could see through the veil.

"Where do you live?" I asked. That was always a good place to start. Sometimes old houses made noises. If it was an old pipe banging around and not a ghost, I could just recommend a good plumber.

"Over on Westfield Drive," she said. "So you'll come?"

"That's over in the new part of town, isn't it?"

"It is," she said. "My house is less than a year old."

Well, that ruled out old house creepiness being the cause. It was also unusual for new houses to be haunted. Whatever was going on, it was enough to arouse my curiosity.

"So, you'll come?" Nora asked again when I didn't respond right away. "I cannot go back there alone. I can't take this anymore."

"Again, no offense, but I'm going to need some more details before I go off alone with you," I said.

"I understand," Nora said before taking a deep shuddering breath. "I don't know what's going on or why this all started. It's not like the house has always been haunted. It was fine up until the last few weeks."

"Okay," I said. "But let's not start there. Let's start with why you came to see me? Why did you think I was the person who would help you with this problem?"

She studied me for a second. "You own the shop down in the square. Is it just a tourist trap? Have I misjudged?" Nora suddenly looked embarrassed. "I just thought that you were into paranormal stuff."

"I am," I said. "My store isn't just a tourist trap, but I do like to know what you know before I say too much."

"I get it," she replied. "There's something different about Coventry. It's not like any other place I've been. I've never been able to put my finger on it, and most people think I'm either crazy or seeing things."

"That happens," I said.

I realized then she was like Thorn. Nora wasn't a witch, but the veil didn't affect her as much. There was no point in trying to hide it from her. Well, the ghost stuff anyway. She didn't seem to know I was a witch, and I didn't need to tell her.

"Why don't you come inside for some tea. We'll talk and figure out what to do," I said.

Chapter Two

So, Nora came in and we, my parents included, all sat around the kitchen table. I made tea and coffee.

Nora greedily glugged down two cups of coffee while it was still hot. She looked like she needed it to keep it from falling over.

The rest of us drank tea. All but Thorn, who stood off in a corner rocking Laney protectively and watching Nora like a hawk. Until the baby needed a diaper change and a bottle. When he reluctantly left, Nora really got started with her story.

"It started with this weird scratching sound," she said. "I called an exterminator and convinced the company that built my house to pay for it."

"I'm guessing that the exterminator didn't find anything," I said.

"I wish," Nora said with a snort. "But what he found didn't have anything to do with scratching. The house is... was infested with spiders. That's taken care of, but like I said, it didn't explain the scratching."

"So what does?" I asked.

"The ghost," Nora replied. "It started out in the kitchen. I'd hear it when I got up early in the morning. Early enough that it was still dark like nighttime outside. I'd be standing in my kitchen making coffee, and it would start under my feet or under the table."

"You have a basement?" I asked.

"I do, and as terrified as I was to check, I did go down there several times. I never found anything that would explain the sound. I mean, that's why I called the exterminator," Nora paused and took a deep breath. "After a week or so, the scratching moved to my bedroom. I'd wake up in the middle of the night and hear it under my bed. That freaked me out so much, but it was worse when it moved into the closet. I would get up and check, and there'd be nothing there. I'd try to go back to sleep, and it would start again. So, I'd check. This goes on all night now."

"No wonder you can't sleep," Mom said.

"It's like it's wearing me down," Nora said.

"That sounds demonic," I replied. "That's what demons do. They wear you down so you are physically and mentally weakened. It makes you easier to possess."

"Oh, no," Nora said. She was already pale, but I watched as the last of the color drained from her face.

"It would explain why it's happening in a new house," I said. "Demons don't care about how old the house is because they aren't like ghosts. They aren't there because they aren't ready to let go. They're there for you."

"Kinsley," Mom said and patted my hand.

I was about to ask her what was wrong, but I looked over at Nora. She was shaking and tears were streaming down her face, but there was something else. It was like she knew and I'd just confirmed her suspicions.

"Is there anything else?" I asked. "It's got to be more than scratching." More evidence might point away from a demon. It was important that I knew everything.

"Things go missing," Nora said. She had her arms wrapped around her waist like she was cold, but she wasn't shaking nearly as much. "I put my keys down on the counter and I can't find them. But after an hour of searching, I'll find them right where I left them. Most of the time. Sometimes I'll find things in strange places."

"That could go either way," I said. "Is there anything else?"

"There's probably a lot more, but I'm having so much trouble remembering things. I'm so exhausted," Nora said, and she looked like she was about to put her head down on my kitchen table and take a nap. "I do smell strange things sometimes. A whiff of flowers out of nowhere, and sometimes something burning."

"Like sulfur?" I asked.

"No. More like burnt toast," Nora yawned and stretched.

"Did you burn your toast?" I asked warily.

"No. My toaster went out. I guess that's another thing. Electronics in my house either dying or not behaving," Nora said.

"So, what brought you here tonight?" I asked. "You said this has been going on for weeks. Did you just get to the point where you're too tired to deal with it anymore? Oh, and did you try staying in a hotel to get some sleep?"

"I did. After about two weeks of sleep deprivation, I stayed in the hotel near my house. The one close to the little strip," Nora said.

"I know the one," I said.

"Something kept tapping on the window all night," she said with a sigh. "Of course, I'd get up and check, and there'd be nothing there. I complained to the night manager in case it was kids messing around, but there was nothing on any of the security cameras. Just me looking out of my room into the parking lot. I thought about calling the police, but what would they do?"

"We would have at least driven by a few times," Thorn said.

He reappeared in the kitchen with Laney. She reached out for me when she saw me, and I took her. Thorn sat down in the empty chair between me and Nora.

"I don't know what good that would have done," Nora said.

"It might have made you feel safer," I suggested.

"Well, if it is a demon, it succeeded in wearing me down, because I don't know that I will ever feel safe again," Nora said. "But I think I'm ready to tell you about why I'm here tonight."

"Let me get you another cup of chamomile tea," I said.

"Valerian," Nora said. "Do you have valerian tea?"

"I do," I said, "but that might put you to sleep."'

"It won't," she assured me. "But unless you've got whiskey, I need something a little stronger than chamomile to get me through this."

"I'll get it," I responded.

Whiskey was a terrible idea for someone in her condition. So, I made her tea, and we all sipped and listened to Nora's story.

She told us how her doorbell rang, and when she went into the living room to answer it, the entity knocked her dinner off her kitchen table. Of course, there was no one at her front door, but when she went back to the kitchen, her bowl of soup was smashed and splattered all over the kitchen floor.

That was about the time the tap in the sink started turning on and off on its own. It would stay off while she tried to wet her rag to clean up the soup, and then turn on by itself when she would walk away.

What started in the kitchen quickly moved through the entire house. She could hear the sinks in the rest of the house turning on and off by themselves.

She left the mess and tried to flee the house, but her front and back door were locked. No matter how many times she tried to throw the deadbolt, it wouldn't disengage.

Following some sort of instinct, she ran for her bedroom. "I tried to hide under the covers," Nora said. "Like I was a little kid hiding from the boogeyman. It made no sense, but it was the only thing my brain would let me do. I was in fight-or-flight mode, and I really couldn't do either."

Nora told us that after she hid in her bed, the house began to shake. At that point, she was sure one of her neighbors would call the police, but I could tell by the way Thorn was shaking his head "no" that no one had called. Nora's neighbors most likely had no idea what was going on in her house. The shaking was real to her but no one else had perceived it.

"And then I wanted to run again," Nora said. "So, I tried to throw off the covers, but I couldn't. They were wrapped around me and tightening like a snake. Like one of those pythons trying to kill its prey. I could barely move, and it felt like I couldn't breathe."

At that point, Nora said she threw herself off the bed with the covers still wrapped around her. She didn't know why, but after a couple more minutes of struggling, she was able to free herself from the blankets.

"It started to lose energy," I said. "These things can only manifest themselves for so long, and while a direct attack like that means we're dealing with something powerful, they still have their limits."

"Is that why you were able to get out?" Dad asked her. "You could open the doors?"

"I could," Nora said. "I remember hearing someone screaming as I ran through the house. It was me. I was in a blind panic as I sprinted for the door. I'd completely forgotten that they wouldn't open before. I'd forgotten everything, but I can tell you with absolute certainty that if that door hadn't opened, I would have thrown myself through my front window. I was like a terrified animal at that point."

"You need to get some sleep," I said. "We'll go to your house in the morning."

"Kinsley," Thorn had a warning edge in his voice. He already knew what I intended.

"She can stay with Mom and Dad," I said. "Right?"

I knew Thorn didn't want me letting a stranger stay in our house. He wouldn't take the risk with Laney around, but I couldn't just send Nora away.

"Shouldn't you look at the house while the entity is still at its weakest?" Dad said. "I'll go with you."

"It's not going to get its strength back overnight," I said. "It would be better if we go during the day. Besides, Nora is too vulnerable right now. She needs some good food and to sleep."

"We'll get her fixed up," Mom said as she stood up from her chair. "Come on, Nora. I've got some leftover cheesy casserole that's delicious reheated and a guest bed."

"What if it comes to your house?" Nora asked. "I can't put you in danger."

"We'll be in no danger, sweetie," Mom said. "It's not going to show back up again tonight, and if it does, my husband... let's just say he can handle things."

Nora seemed a bit reluctant at first, but you could tell that she'd have done just about anything for some sleep. Mom texted me when they got home that Nora'd fallen asleep in the car, but that she'd woken up enough to eat.

Mom had also gotten her to take a shower and put on fresh pajamas. Something had happened at Nora's house that she was afraid to take a shower, but she'd left that part out of her story.

Either way, Mom stood outside of the guest bathroom while Nora showered. They'd left the door open a crack, so that whenever Nora called out, Mom could reassure her she was right there.

That night, I only dozed on the sofa with Laney in the playpen next to me. It might have just been my imagination, but after Thorn went to sleep, I could have sworn I heard scratching coming from my bedroom closet.

Chapter Three

The next morning, Dad brought Nora back over to my house to pick me up. Thorn had wanted to come too, but he'd resigned himself to staying home with Laney.

"We'll drop her off with Mom," I said when he looked beyond exasperated. "But really, the three of us will be fine."

"I should have brought your mother," Dad said.

"It's fine," I said. "You and Nora go to the house. Thorn and I will drop off Laney, and we'll be right there."

So, that's what we did. Meri was torn between going with me or staying with Laney. It was as if a heavy decision had to be made, and the outcome would have far-reaching consequences.

But in the end, he came with me. I was surprised, and so was Mom. He'd left being her familiar so quickly when I was born, and we'd all assumed he'd do the same with Laney.

"Don't make it weird," Meri said as we all got back into the car.

"You're still my familiar," I said.

"Whatever," was his response before he went back to staring out the window.

"I actually think I'd feel better if she had a familiar to protect her," Thorn said as we drove to Nora's house.

"If that's what is to be, then a familiar will come to her," I said.

"One never came to your mother," Thorn said. "After Meri became yours."

"Because it wasn't meant to be," I said. "Not all witches have familiars."

"I know I heard a story about you guys turning a woman into a pig and making her a familiar," Thorn said.

"That wasn't me," I retorted. "So you want us to turn someone into a familiar for Laney?"

"I mean, can't we just go to the pound and get a cat... or maybe a puppy?"

"That's not how it works," I said. "And even if the Coven had the power at one time to make a familiar, we don't right now. At least, not one you'd want around your daughter."

"So, we wait?" Thorn asked.

"When it comes to this, that's all we can do," I said.

"What about this ghost or demon thing? You guys have the magic to fight off something like this? I mean, why are you getting involved?" Thorn asked.

"Because you saw her," I said. "She's completely desperate and in real danger."

"You said yourself that this entity is powerful," Thorn said.

"So if push comes to shove, we'll fight fire with fire," I said.

"I'm not sure how I feel about you guys using all this dark magic just because it still works," Thorn said.

"I thought you loved me because I am both," I said, and it took me back to the moment when Azriel told me he loved me because of my darkness. I shook the memory off like I was shaking off a chill.

"I love you no matter what, Kinsley," Thorn said. "But it concerns me that you're so readily embracing dark things. Won't spending so much time and energy on black arts have... I don't know… some effect on you? Won't it leave a mark on your soul?"

"I won't let that happen," I said. "I will get this magic thing figured out, and then I can go back to using regular old white magic. Maybe a little gray too, but Thorn, I can't just not be a witch. I know that's what I always wanted, but there is too much at stake."

"That doesn't mean you need to help this woman. You don't need to put your soul at risk for a stranger," Thorn said. "Not when we have a little girl to raise."

"So, what would you have me do? Leave her stranded? Let whatever is in her house kill her or possess her?" I asked.

"You could let your parents handle it," Thorn said. "Heck, you could let any number of witches in this town do this. It doesn't have to be you."

"I thought we'd already been over this, Thorn. I thought you were okay with me being me and all that," I said.

"This is different," Thorn said.

"How is it different?" I asked. "I mean, there's no body this time. So, I'm not investigating a murder. I thought you'd support that."

He just glanced over at me without saying a word. I saw his jaw tighten and then Thorn swallowed hard. But he didn't say anything else.

"My magic has been reduced, but I'm not powerless," I said. "And I really do think that I'm getting stronger again."

"You're going to try to use white magic to solve whatever this is?" Thorn asked and squeezed my hand.

"Of course," I said. "I've used darker magic when I had to help people I loved, but it's not like I'm embracing it. I don't want to be a dark witch."

"Because I've heard the stories," Thorn said, and I knew what he was talking about.

"About my dad," I said. "He let too much of it in…"

"And that's what I'm worried about happening to you," Thorn said. "You're Brighton's daughter, but you're Remy's too. Some of that susceptibility is in you."

My father had gotten a little too snuggly with dark magic before he and my mother became a couple. He'd done it to protect those he loved, but he'd still let too much in. His eyes turned black, and he actually stalked my mom for a while.

Fortunately, she understood what happened to him and forgave him. If she hadn't, I wouldn't even exist.

"Are you worried about me being susceptible or inclined?" I asked.

"I'm not trying to make this some sort of moral failing on your part," Thorn said, but he took his hand back and put it on the steering wheel. He was clearly distancing himself from me because we didn't need to do anything to drive the car.

It was quiet the rest of the way to my parents' house. When we got there, I started to get out but Thorn stopped me.

"I'll take Laney up to your mother," he said and got out of the car before I could respond.

I watched as Thorn went up to Mom's door, rang the bell and waited. She answered, and they had a short conversation followed by my mother taking Laney into her arms. My baby was laughing and smiling, so something in my chest unclenched.

Thorn walked down the porch and back to the car. "I'm sorry," he said as he slid into the driver's side. "I trust you to handle this, and I shouldn't question why you need to do it."

"And I understand why you're scared," I said as he took my hand. "But I can handle this. Please understand that it's more than just helping Nora too. I mean, I want to help her, but there's also something wrong with magic. Something wrong with witches. I have to follow every lead and turn over every stone until I find it. I just don't have a lot to go on."

"And you think the magic issues might have something to do with Nora's ghost?" Thorn asked as the car drove us toward her address.

"I don't know," I answered. "And I won't until I check it out. If not, then at least we helped a distressed woman along the way."

"Well, let's do that then," Thorn said.

We arrived at Nora's house to find her and my father standing in the driveway. It was wide and led up to a three-car garage. The house itself was a ranch, and I guessed from its shape, and what was popular at the time, it was split-level.

I wondered what Nora did for a living because the house was at least 3,000 square feet, if not approaching four. The front façade was mostly stone with some brick accents. The color scheme was rich chocolate brown with earthy beiges and the occasional pop of red.

"This house is beautiful," I said as we made our way up the sidewalk to the front porch area.

"Thank you," Nora said. "I bought it as new construction, and I got to pick out a lot of the finishes. I'm glad you think it's nice. So many people around here were going with black, white, and gray. I wasn't sure how well the earth tones would go over."

"I think it's lovely," Dad said. "Nothing wrong with being a little different."

"I guess that's especially true around here," Nora said.

By that point, the four of us were gathered on her front porch in front of a large window. We couldn't see inside the house because the shades were closed.

"I don't know if I want to go in," Nora said.

"That's understandable, but we need you to show us around," I said. "It will be okay, and if it gets scary again, we'll get you out."

Nora didn't say anything more to that, but she nodded her head in affirmation. I watched as she turned around and unlocked the deadbolt with her key.

For a moment, I wondered if it would even open. Would the spirit inside let us in? My magic wasn't what it once was, but I could still get the door open if it came to that. I'd been working for the last few months to strengthen my powers. It turned out that our abilities were like muscles, and I could get better with practice.

"You brought your cat," Nora said as she opened the door and Meri darted inside.

It seemed like the first time she'd noticed him, but he'd been standing next to my leg. "I did," I responded. "He's sensitive to spirits. Most cats are. If there's anything around, he'll pick up on it before we will."

That wasn't necessarily true, but I didn't want to explain to her Meri's true nature. I'd decided earlier that I wasn't going to discuss or reveal anything about witchcraft to Nora unless I absolutely had to tell her. If we could leave it at whatever she'd picked up in my shop, that would be better.

I'm not sure what I was expecting, but when we stepped over the threshold, the house just felt like a house. It was clean and bright with a fresh lemon smell.

"Wow," I said as I walked around the massive living room just past the entryway. "This is really gorgeous."

"It really is," my dad added.

Thorn was sort of making his way toward the kitchen area. I called it a kitchen area because the house's floorplan was completely open and the kitchen flowed into the living room. At the back of the house was a large dining area with a massive twelve-person table.

"You live alone?" I asked as I studied the table.

"I do," Nora said with a nervous chuckle. "I know the table is a lot, but it was my grandmother's. It fits in so well here, in fact I chose the color palate around it, that I had to use it. Maybe someday I'll have enough people over to fill the seats."

That was something I hadn't thought of before. While the house was brand new, there could be objects inside with entities attached.

Nora had lived in the house for months, though. Surely any spirits attached to her antique furniture would have begun manifesting previously. They might have even been restless wherever she lived before.

"Did you just bring the table into the house?" I asked. "Where did it come from?"

"It was in my parents' storage," Nora replied. "My old house wasn't big enough for anything like it, but it's been here since the day I moved in."

Well, that probably wasn't it, then. "What about new antiques? Have you purchased anything recently? Does the… activity coincide with any new objects you brought into the house?"

Nora thought about it for a moment. She bit her bottom lip as she mulled it over in her head. "Nothing I can think of recently. Almost everything I purchased for the house was either before I moved in or right after. I think the only things I've bought for the last couple of months are groceries. Come to think of it, I've been so busy with work that I haven't been doing my usual Amazon ordering. I bet the UPS guy thinks I'm dead," she said with a nervous laugh.

"What do you do for work?" I asked.

"I'm a data scientist," Nora said.

"Well, that doesn't sound like anything that would attract ghosts," Dad said.

"Dad," I scolded.

"He's right," Nora said with a smile. "I won't bore you with the details, but I work on machine-learning algorithms. It's actually one of the reasons I bought this house. I was working in the city, but it was too hard for me to concentrate with a bunch of people around. When my team and I started to get into some seriously deep work, I asked for permission to work from home. The I realized that if I was going to work from home, I wanted something big, spacious, and full of light. I live here alone, but that just means I can use one of the bedrooms as a music room and another as a workout room."

My eyes flitted over to a staircase that descended from the main floor. "You have a basement here?"

"I do, and I had them finish it. One of the rooms has an infinity pool so I can swim laps year-round. There's also an entertaining space and a bar."

"This house has everything," I said.

"It has a little more than I bargained for," Nora replied.

"Could you just walk me through the areas of the house where you heard the scratching?" I asked.

Nora walked us through the kitchen and then down a short hallway that led to the master bedroom. It was the room where she'd not only heard the scratching, but the bedroom was also where the main attack occurred.

I stood in the middle of the room next to Nora's king-sized bed. She stayed in the doorway observing me, but I could tell she wasn't coming in. It was too bad.

I couldn't imagine what she'd paid for the place. She'd put all of her personal touches on it too, and at that point, Nora no longer wanted anything to do with the house.

"Anything happen in the bathroom?" I asked. Mostly because I wanted to check it out, and I felt weird about walking into her bathroom for no reason. It had to be gorgeous, though.

"No," she said. "Wait, sometimes I did feel like I was being watched in there. When I was in the shower. I don't know. Maybe the ghost was a perv."

"It's not unusual," Dad said. "Not that ghosts are pervs, but that people feel like they are being watched in the shower. Most of the time, it's just because we feel so vulnerable when we are bathing, and it's not actually anything watching us."

"Oh, well, that's good to know," Nora said.

"Do you mind if I have a look anyway?" I asked.

"Sure, go ahead. My housekeepers were just here a day or so ago. I don't know. When I get deep into my work, it all runs together," Nora said. "But either way, it's not embarrassing in there yet."

"You have housekeepers?" I asked. "Have they observed anything strange in the house?"

"I don't think so," Nora replied. "They don't talk to me much, but neither of them have acted like anything was unusual. They haven't run out of here in terror or anything,"

Thorn had come into the room with me, but he'd been looking out the bedroom's largest window the entire time. He finally said something at the mention of the housekeepers and Nora's work. "You told us that you'd barely been sleeping. How could you have been so deep in your work that you don't know what day it is too?" Thorn asked. He'd picked up on a possible inconsistency that I hadn't. "No offense, but you came to us because you're a mess. How have you been working at all?"

"You're right," Nora said. "It's been a struggle, but my project has to keep moving forward. I've been doing what I can, and my team checks my work. It's not like it's the first time I've had to work on little sleep."

Thorn nodded. He knew what that was like too, and apparently, her answer had satisfied him.

I wasn't sure what to do at that point. "Are you picking up on anything, Dad?" I asked. I wanted to ask Meri the same thing, but not only was he not in the room with us, he wouldn't be able to answer me anyway. Why I had a talking cat, or even why I was talking to my not-talking cat, wasn't a conversation I wanted to have with Nora.

"Nothing," he said. "Oddly so given everything that's gone on here. You'd think there'd be some residue."

"Residue?" Nora asked.

"Yeah. When that much paranormal activity goes on in a place, it leaves behind a residue. Given what you've told us happened here, this place had to have been swimming in spectral energy," I said.

"And yet, it's like nothing," Dad said. "Not even an off vibration. There's nowhere in Coventry that's this clean."

Nora shivered. "Give me a second. I'm going to go turn down the air conditioning. I guess I got a little overzealous with it. We're supposed to get that big warm-up, though."

The hair on the back of my neck stood up. The room had turned suddenly chilly, and I didn't believe for a second that it was the air conditioning.

"A calm before the storm," I said and swallowed hard.

"What?" Dad asked, but I could see in his eyes that the same conclusion was dawning on him too.

"The lack of energy, it was a calm before the storm," I said. "I didn't think whatever it was could come back, but it's drawing every little bit of available energy."

"What?" Nora asked.

"Scraping the bottom of the barrel," Dad said. "Something is about to happen."

"We should get out of here," Nora whispered.

"We'll be okay," I said. "If it's working this hard just to appear, then it's not going to hurt us."

"It can't," Dad said.

"Are you sure?" Nora's voice cracked. She sounded as if she were on the edge of hysterics, and I noticed she was slowly backing down the hallway half a step at a time.

"Nora, stay with us," I said, and then I saw it. "Stop backing up right now."

She could see me looking over her shoulder. Nora turned and screamed.

"Oh, now that's creepy," Thorn said.

In the hallway was the ghost of a woman, but she barely looked human. Her eyes were completely black, and her skin looked mottled and gray. It was the eyes, though, that had me questioning whether we were looking at a ghost or a demon doing a bad impression of a person.

"Get back," I said and stepped around Nora.

My first instinct was to put myself between the specter and everyone else. Meri did the same, except he stood protectively before me.

It would have been great if we still had the magic we once held. Meri could have dispatched the ghost, or demon, in seconds. I thought he still could sometimes, so I wondered why he was sitting there staring at the thing.

Are you going to do something about her? I wanted to ask Meri, but I couldn't. Part of me started to wish I'd listened to Thorn and stayed home.

Obviously, if there was something Meri could do about the ghost, he would have done it. But instead, he looked back at me and then at the ghost. He did that a couple more times, and then approached her.

"Meri," I said almost breathlessly. It wasn't that I expected him to respond, but I hoped he'd listen and not follow the specter.

When he approached her, the ghost turned and began to move down the hall. Meri looked back at me again, and I knew what he wanted.

So, I started to follow too. It felt insane. The woman, or demon disguised as a woman, was absolutely terrifying. And yet, Meri didn't seem to be afraid.

She led us to a door just past the kitchen before you got to the two smaller bedrooms. "What's this door?" I asked Nora.

The ghost had stopped and seemed to be patiently waiting. She turned to look at us, and her skin was whiter than gray. The black had cleared from her eyes and the irises were a soft shade of hazel.

"It's the basement door," Nora said.

The ghost moved through it, and I reached out and opened the door. "I guess we're going to the basement."

"You're really going to follow it down there?" Nora asked. Judging by the tone of her voice, she was horrified.

"We came here to figure out what was going on with your house," I said. "I think this is the best way to do it."

"She attacked me," Nora said. "That thing could have killed me."

"And she seems to have something to tell us," I said. "Maybe if we find out what that is, she'll move on. I'm starting to think that she's not a demon but an angry spirit. That can happen to anyone if they are left to linger on this plane in confusion."

"Or she could be a demon deceiving us," Dad said.

"I'm aware, but we'll be careful," I said.

"How is going down there being careful?" Nora's question was shrill and full of terror.

"Or we can go," I said. "I'm not really sure what you want me to do."

"Can't you do like a séance or something?" Nora asked. "Make her appear up here in the safety of a protection circle. I could help you cast it. And then you can get rid of her from there."

Dad and I exchanged glances.

"That would be a lot of work to manifest a spirit that's already here and trying to show us what it wants," I said. "And if it's a demon, it might reveal its weakness. We just have to watch it carefully."

A shiver ran through me when I looked down the basement stairs. The ghost stood at the bottom looking up at me. I hadn't turned the light on yet, so she peered up at me from the inky blackness.

My hand searched the wall and found the switch. When I turned it on, the ghost turned too and began to drift into the basement.

I held the rail and made my way down the steps quickly. They were carpeted in plush gray that was soft underfoot and muffled any sound of our descent.

When I got to the bottom, I looked around. For the life of me, I couldn't figure out why Nora had been afraid to come down to the basement. Once you had the lights on, it wasn't some creepy dark hole in the ground with a concrete or dirt floor. The basement was just as nice as the rest of the house. It even had several egress windows in the bedrooms that let in some natural light once you got past the main room.

But the ghost drifted past all of that. She made her way to the door that led to the unfinished utility area of the basement.

We went inside and followed her past the furnace and sump pump. On the other side, we found another door.

"What's this?" I asked.

"It leads to an unfinished part of the basement," Nora said.

"We're in the unfinished part of the basement," I shot back.

"I guess it's more of a crawlspace," she said. "I don't know. I don't really go in there."

"Why did you need a crawlspace under your house if you've got both finished and unfinished basement?" I asked.

"It was in the plans for the house, and I didn't really mind it," Nora said. "I think it's because the basement isn't quite as big as the house above."

I turned the knob and pushed the door open. Light flooded into the crawlspace from the basement, and it illuminated the room enough for me to see a bulb and chain in the middle. I walked into the room and pulled the chain.

The crawlspace was just another section of unfinished basement with a dirt floor. Its presence made zero sense, and I had to wonder if the builder had just done it to cut corners and costs.

"What about the ghost?" Dad asked as I stood there contemplating the crawlspace.

"Right. The reason we're here. Why are we here?" I asked the specter.

I didn't want to speak to her in case she was a demon. Acknowledging them was a sure way to let them into your world, but we'd already followed her down to the basement. That ship had sailed already.

The ghost just remained in the same spot staring at me. Finally, a soft, scratchy whisper came from her direction. "Here," she said. And then she vanished. The ghost had used up every bit of energy she could draw from to utter that word, and I was sure she wasn't coming back anytime soon. I'd thought she would have been spent from the night before, but at that point, I was sure there was nothing else she could do. Anger, and perhaps I'd seen a hint of fear too, would only get her so far.

"What does she mean?" Nora asked. "What did she mean by here?"

"I don't know," I said, but I walked over to the spot where she'd vanished.

Meri joined me, and we stood there studying the floor for a moment. "The dirt's different here," I finally said.

"What do you mean?" Dad asked. He and Thorn joined me at the spot. They both stood there staring at the dirt floor beneath our feet.

"She's right," Thorn finally said. "See, it's raised up just a little higher than the dirt around it. Step back," he said taking on his authoritative sheriff voice.

"Do you have a shovel?" I asked Nora.

"Out in the garage," she said.

"Could you go get it?" I asked.

"I should... I don't know. Should I call for backup?" Thorn asked.

"For what?" I asked. "We don't know what's down there yet."

"Can't be anything good," Meri snarked since Nora was out of the room grabbing a shovel.

"I'm going to call it in," Thorn said.

"Call in what?" I asked. "I don't know. Something isn't right, though. I can feel it."

"We can all feel it," Dad said. "Just give it a few minutes, son."

Nora returned shortly after that with the shovel. At that point, Thorn stood off to my side suspiciously watching the hole. He wasn't a witch, but I didn't for a second doubt his intuition. He'd always been able to see through the veil that covered Coventry, and that meant Thorn could see things others could not.

My father had wandered out to the bigger unfinished area of the basement, but he returned with Nora. She stood there for a moment looking between us, but it didn't take long for Thorn to reach out and take the shovel.

"I can do that," Dad said.

"So can I," I added.

"Let me," Thorn said calmly. "It will let me feel like I'm contributing."

Nora looked puzzled by his statement, but she didn't say anything about it. Instead, she started to play host. "Does anybody need a drink? It will help me feel like I'm contributing something."

"I'm probably going to need some water," Thorn said as he scooped up another shovelful of the dirt.

"Some water would be good," I said.

"You guys don't think that ghost is going to come back when I'm away from you, do you?" Nora asked. "I felt a bit creeped out when I was in the garage, but I hadn't turned the light on, so I'm pretty sure that's why."

"I don't think she's coming back any time soon… if ever," Dad said. "But I'll go up with you to get the water if it will make you feel safer."

Nora nodded to Dad, and they left to get the water. I turned my attention back to Thorn's digging. Meri sat right at the edge of the hole peering down into it. You'd have thought he was in Thorn's way, but he'd somehow managed to position himself in just the right spot.

Thorn didn't have to dig much farther. Nora walked into the room with two bottles of Fiji water, and she gasped. She also dropped the bottles, and Dad caught them.

My husband stepped away from the hole he'd just dug and took out his phone. "I can't get any reception in here. I'll need to go upstairs. You guys should come with me."

"Are you okay?" I asked as we trudged up the basement stairs. He had a look on his face. Thorn's jaw was set and his eyes narrowed.

"I told you I should have called it in," he said. "We should have had a forensics crew come out here and dig that hole. None of us should have been in there. We've completely trounced all over a crime scene."

"Do you think they would have come?" I asked. "Do you think the forensics people would have come here and dug that hole based on just our gut feelings?"

"You're right," Thorn relented.

"What do I do?" Nora asked. "They're going to come in here and dig up my basement. Am I a suspect?"

"I'm not entirely sure what to make of that," Thorn said. "How long have you lived here?"

"Just a few months," Nora said.

"So even if you killed someone and buried them when you moved in, I'm not entirely sure that's enough time for them to skeletonize," Thorn said. "I'm not an expert, though."

"Someone brought the skeleton into the house and buried it in my crawlspace?" Nora asked.

"Probably when the house was being built," Thorn said. "Someone snuck onto the construction site and buried it here."

"But then why did the ghost just start bothering her?" I asked. "If the skeleton has been here since she moved in, then why did this start recently?"

Thorn thought about it for a minute. "I'm going to need a list of everyone who has been in your house recently," Thorn said. "I especially need to know if you had anyone in here around the time the activity started. Were you having any work done on the house? Any upgrades?"

"I've had people in and out," Nora said. "There have been a lot of problems with this house even starting back during construction. I've had contractors in frequently."

"I'm going to need a list of their names, and if not, at least who they worked for," Thorn said.

"I have receipts and work orders for everything," Nora said. "The builder is responsible for paying me back for all of it, so I've kept meticulous records."

"Why don't you gather that up?" Thorn said to Nora. "Remy, can you take Kinsley home?"

"I'm not going home," I said.

"It would be best," Thorn said. "For the investigation. Please."

"What if she comes back?" Nora whispered so anyone around us didn't hear her. "I can't be here alone."

"She's not coming back," Dad said. "She wanted you to find those bones, and you did. Can you feel the difference in the house? I can. It's like there was a darkness around the edges… a heaviness… that I didn't notice until it was gone, but it is gone."

"He's right," I said. "But you can always go stay with someone if you're not sure. You could rent a room at the motel or the bed and breakfast near the square."

Nora looked around as if noticing the house for the first time. "You're right. It does feel different in here. It feels lighter. I'd swear the lights are even brighter."

"Nothing's sucking the energy out of the place," I said.

Just then, a couple of deputies came through the front door. They propped it open. I assumed that was in anticipation of the forensics team arriving with their equipment.

"I'll go with Dad," I said. "Nora, you can call me if you need to talk. And please, stop into the shop anytime. I'm sure we've got some stuff that will make you feel safer at home and will accentuate the positive energy in here."

"Was that a sales pitch?" Dad asked as we walked out to his car.

"Too much?" I asked.

"I think it was just right," Dad replied.

Chapter Four

Laney was sleeping when I called Mom to tell her that Dad was bringing me to pick her up. She wasn't quite ready to let her granddaughter go either, so we decided I would go home and they'd bring Laney to me later. Or, Thorn could pick her up when he was done working.

So, I was free. I had at least a few hours to do whatever I wanted.

I looked around the house and saw that it was already spotless. I spent so much of my time when Laney was napping cleaning that I didn't have a thing to do as far as chores.

"I have no idea," I said.

"What are you on about?" Meri asked. He'd jumped up on the coffee table and was watching me pace in the living room.

"I have free time," I said. "To myself. I haven't had that in forever, and I have no idea what to do with it."

"Maybe you should work on your magic," Meri suggested. "You could use the practice."

"I think I'm going to go see Dorian," I said.

"Of course you are," Meri snarked.

"You can stay here if you want," I said.

"I could use a nap," Meri said and stretched.

"'Kay. See you later," I said and headed for the front door.

"I'm coming with you," Meri said and jumped down off the coffee table.

On my way over to Dorian and Isaac's house, I sent him a text that I was coming, but he didn't answer. I didn't let that deter me, though.

I pulled into his driveway and got out of the car. Meri hopped out of the driver's side behind me before I shut the door.

After making my way up his front walk and ringing the bell, I waited on the front porch for him to answer. It took a minute for him to get to the door, and had it not been for his car in the driveway ahead of mine, I might have thought he wasn't there.

"Maybe's he's out on a walk," I whispered to Meri as we waited.

Eventually, Dorian answered. His hair was partially sticking up like he'd been running his hands through it over and over, and his eyes were rimmed in red.

"What's the matter," I asked. "Dorian, what's wrong? Is it Isaac?"

"No," he said and began to sob. "It's Buffy. Oh, gawd, Buffy..."

I was thoroughly confused.

"Who is Buffy?" I asked.

"Come in," Dorian said and motioned for me to come through the door. "I need to be watching my phone."

As soon as I was inside, Dorian shut the door and hurried over to his coffee table. He picked up his phone and studied it intensely.

"What's going on?" I asked again since I still hadn't gotten an answer from him.

"Buffy is Isaac's dog," Dorian said. "Well, I guess she's my dog too, but she was his idea. Plus, the dog likes him way more than she likes me. Turns out it was for a good reason." At that, he let out a strangled sob and fresh streams of tears released from his eyes. "Isaac is going to kill me. He's going to be devastated."

"Where is Buffy?" I asked as calmly as possible.

"I don't know," Dorian wailed.

"Dorian, you have to pull yourself together. You are a journalist. You've handled far worse things than a missing dog. Tell me what happened, and we'll fix this," I said. "But get it together, dude."

"I don't know," Meri said. "This is pretty amusing."

"Ugh. Sometimes I forget you have a talking cat," Dorian said.

But the effect was immediate. Meri and his snarky butt had gotten Dorian to stop crying. Thank goodness Dorian had been a werewolf at one time and could handle the whole witch thing. I tried not to think about how exhausting it would have been to have had to keep it hidden from him for our entire lives.

"I do have a talking cat," I said. "And I think we'd both really like it if you'd tell us more about Buffy."

"I lost her on a walk today," Dorian said. "I thought Isaac would be so happy that I took her out for a long walk at the new dog park, but when we were getting back into the car, she pulled away from me and ran into the woods."

"The woods by the dog park?" I asked. "Sorry, I know that sounds like dumb question, but I'm thinking out loud."

"Yes, she shot off like a woman on a mission," Dorian said with a sad chuckle.

"What kind of dog is she?" I asked.

"She's a little white cairn terrier," Dorian said and ran his hands down his face. "Cute little thing, but high energy. When you had the baby, Isaac started to get... I don't know... restless? For a couple of days there, I really thought he was going to suggest we adopt a baby. But then he found the ad for this litter of little puppies. I couldn't tell him no. Buffy is so smart. I don't understand why she'd do this."

"The cairn terrier part explains everything," I said.

"It does?"

"I'm surprised a journalist like you didn't do any research into the dog breed before you got her," I said.

"I didn't," Dorian responded. "I should have. But you're here now, so tell me."

"Cairn terriers have a high prey drive. They love to hunt. She might have focused in on a squirrel or something. Or there's a campground on the other side of those woods. Maybe she heard people and smelled cooking food," I said.

"Well, I've got to try again," Dorian said. "You're lucky you caught me when you did. I just came back here to get more of her favorite treats and another of her toys. I looked for hours. We left for the walk right after Isaac left to help Viv in the coffee shop. It was supposed to be his day off, but once he was up, Buffy was up. I thought maybe after a long walk, she'd let me take a nap. Oh, well. I gotta go. I have to find her before something happens..."

"I'll go with you," I said. "We'll look together."

"Is there anything you can do?" Dorian asked as he picked up a stuffed llama from the floor. "You know... with magic?"

"I could try a tracking spell," I said. "But given the way my powers are working, it would take a while to pull it all together. It's probably better for us to get back out there and look. We should save the magical solution for if all else fails."

"Come on," Dorian said. "We're taking my car."

Dorian pulled into the parking lot at the dog park, and I immediately began looking for little white terriers. "Maybe you should stay in the car," I said to Meri.

He seemed eager to get out of Dorian's car, and I wasn't sure it was a good idea. There weren't that many dogs there, but the sight of a cat could have started pandemonium. Meri's solution was to climb into my purse. He'd definitely gotten a little bigger, but he still fit.

"You were here in the parking lot when she got away?" I asked.

"Yes, right here in this spot," Dorian said. "I had just unclipped her leash so I could fasten her harness to the safety seat, and she leapt out of the seat and took off that way." He pointed toward a small opening in the trees.

"All right, bring the treats and the toy. Also keep an eye out around the dog park. She might have come back and been confused because you weren't here," I said.

"Oh, no," Dorian moaned. "I shouldn't have left. I knew it."

"You were looking for hours," I said. "You were going to have to leave at some point, but if we don't find her soon, we're going to need to call Isaac. Maybe if he comes out here too, she'll turn up."

"You mean like she'll come to him even if she won't come to me," Dorian said.

"I mean, I didn't say it that way," I said and bit my lip.

"It's fine," Dorian said. "I know I'm not her person. Isaac's never going to forgive me if we don't find her," Dorian said.

"Yes, he would," I said. "But we're going to find her."

By that time, we'd made it across the grass to the trees. Since no one was around, and it didn't appear that any of the people at the dog park were paying attention, I took Meri out of my purse and put him on the ground. He shot off into the woods so fast he looked like a black blur.

"You think he's going to find her?" Dorian said hopefully.

"I bet he's already picked up her scent. Let's try to follow in the direction he went. If we can figure that out..." I said.

"What if we can't find him too?" Dorian asked.

"He'll lead her back to us," I said. "You have her leash?"

"I do," Dorian said. He had her leash in one hand, her llama in the other, and a bag of treats stuffed in each pocket.

None of that was necessary, though. The way Meri took off, I knew he'd already found Buffy. I just hoped that she was all right.

We trudged through the woods without talking to one another. Dorian frequently called out for Buffy. I kept quiet, though. I thought my voice might be unfamiliar to her since we hadn't met yet.

Instead, I paid attention to the trees. I'd heard them whispering before, but I didn't know if I could anymore. Trees would talk to witches if they listened, but it was a skill you had to sharpen. It was one I'd neglected because I'd fancied myself more of the crystal and potion type of witch.

Which was funny because I'd hardly made any potions in my life. Nothing even coming close to other witches of my age. I should have worked harder. If I had, I probably could have thrown together a tracking potion at Dorian's house with what he had in his pantry. I knew there were witches in the family Coven who could do something like that in minutes, and before the reset, they'd been far less powerful than me.

Hard work and practice always trump talent without practice.

"Anything?" I asked when I got tired of lamenting my own failings. "Any streaks of white?"

"Nothing yet," Dorian said and called out "Buffy!" again.

The trees were hard to hear, but if I was correct, they were guiding us in the right direction. Good old trees. They didn't care that I'd neglected my magical studies and powers. All they cared about was that in that moment, I was ready to listen.

"We're going in the right direction," I practically whispered to Dorian. "The trees say so."

"You can talk to trees?" Dorian asked.

"I can hear them," I said. "It's not something I used much before, but I can definitely hear them."

"What are they telling you?" Dorian asked hopefully.

"It's more that they are guiding us," I said. "They aren't speaking in words like us. It's more like they are communicating ideas, and what they are telling me right now is that we are about to find something."

"Buffy?" Dorian asked.

"I hope so," I said. "Let's just keep going."

We walked for a few more minutes, and I could see what looked like a clearing up ahead. I picked up the pace and called out for Meri. We hadn't seen him since he'd taken off into the woods.

"There's an opening ahead," Dorian said.

"Maybe we've made it to the campground," I said. "Perhaps someone there found her and is holding onto her."

"I hope nobody tries to steal her," Dorian said. "She's a purebred and so sweet."

"If someone's got her in their camper, we'll know," I said. "She'll bark like crazy if she hears you."

"You're right," Dorian said, and I could see him relax a little.

The clearing turned out to be an open space. There was no one camping in it currently, but we'd definitely made it to the grounds.

The campsites were not stacked on top of each other. There were sections of trees in between each to give campers privacy and that sense of being alone in the woods. Some of the sites were for RVs and others were for tents. The one Dorian and I had come upon was smaller and didn't have a driveway for an RV.

"Let's keep going," I said.

As soon as we were back in the trees, Dorian grabbed my shoulder. "What's that?" he asked.

"What's what?" But when I looked around, I saw it.

There was a hole dug between two big oak trees. Meri sat perched on the edge looking down.

"Buffy?" Dorian called out frantically.

For the longest second of my life, the forest around us was almost completely silent. Then the air filled with the sound of frantic barking.

"Buffy!" Dorian called out.

We ran over to the hole and found Buffy at the bottom of a shallow pit. She was caked with dirt and mud and wagged her tail proudly.

"She's all right," I said and Dorian scooped her up.

"Filthy… But yes, she seems to be okay," Dorian said.

I looked into the hole. It was big enough that she wasn't able to climb back out, but it wasn't so deep that she'd been injured when, I assumed, she fell in.

"Well, let's get her home so you can give her a bath before Isaac sees her like that," I said with a relieved chuckle.

"Kinsley?" Dorian asked as he attached Buffy's leash to her harness and double-checked it.

"Yeah?" I responded.

"I mean, don't get me wrong. I want to get Buffy home, and I'm so glad we found her, but don't you wonder what this hole is? I mean, I'm trying to shut off my reporter brain, but I can't… This is kind of weird, right?" Dorian asked.

I hadn't thought about it because I was so glad we'd found his dog. He was right, though.

The large but shallow rectangular hole in the woods was a little strange.

"It kinda looks like..." I trailed off because I didn't want to say it.

"It looks like a shallow grave, right?" Dorian finished the thought for me.

"That's what it looks like," I said.

It was then that I spotted something in the dirt. During her time in the hole, Buffy had dug down a few inches in some spots. Sticking out of one of them was something white.

"What is that?" I asked.

"I'm going to take some pictures of this," Dorian said. He managed to get his phone out and snap some photos while holding Buffy under his other arm. "I'm going to take a little video too, so stay back if you don't want to be in it."

But I wasn't paying any attention. He was shooting video, and I knelt at the side of the hole next to Meri.

"Don't," Meri hissed as I reached out for the white object.

My head snapped up. I'd been sort of mesmerized by the object, but Meri broke the spell. I thought I saw someone off in the distance in the trees.

She was gone before I could wrap my head around her presence. I rubbed my eyes and looked again, but the ghost of the woman in Nora's house didn't reappear. I could have sworn I saw her, though. Was my mind playing tricks on me?

I turned my attention back to the white object in the hole. Dorian walked over and stood on the other side. "Is that..." he started to ask, but stopped when I stood up.

"I'm going to walk into the clearing and see if I can get a signal on my phone," I said.

I pulled it out and didn't have anything under the trees, but thankfully, once I was in the open, I got a strong signal. "Thorn," I said when he picked up the call.

"What is it?" he asked. "Is Laney okay?"

"Laney's fine," I said. "She's still with my mom and dad. She was asleep when I got there, so Mom wanted to keep her for a while. I figured you could pick her up when you're done with the crime scene. Or I can have them bring her home if you've got a lot of paperwork."

"I'm glad you're understanding about this. I know it's supposed to be my day off," Thorn said.

"Of course," I answered. "You're actually only working because of me, so how could I be mad?"

"Thank you," he said. "So, are you at home then? Getting some rest maybe?"

"About that," I started. "So, I went to go visit Dorian. You know I haven't seen him much since Laney was born, and I figured it was a good time for a visit. Anyway, he was pretty distraught because he and Isaac got a dog, and he lost it on a morning walk. I went with him to look for Buffy."

"Oh," Thorn said. "Do you want me to have my deputies keep an eye out?"

"No, thanks though. That's the good news. We found Buffy, but I need to ask you something."

"Go ahead," Thorn said with a nervous chuckle. "You're being awfully cryptic, my love."

"The skeleton we found at Nora's house. You've had a better chance to look at it now, and I was wondering if it's missing a finger?"

"It is…" Thorn said cautiously. "Why?"

"Well, I think we might have found where she was buried before," I said. "There's a hole here with a skeleton finger in it. It's near the dog park where we found Buffy. You might want to send the forensics team over here."

He sighed heavily. "Can you send me your location? Use the GPS in your phone."

"I can do that," I said.

"And then, Kinsley?"

"Yeah, babe?"

"I love you, but go home. Please," Thorn said.

"I love you too, and I think I'm going to go with Dorian and help him give Buffy a bath. She's very dirty."

"Good enough for me," Thorn said.

Chapter Five

Dorian was glad to have me there to help bathe Buffy. She was not happy about it at all, though. Thankfully, she tolerated Meri's presence because he sat on the sink and watched the entire event unfold.

Buffy did not want a bath. She fussed and fought us so hard that a tidal wave began to surge from one end of the bathtub to the other. It mostly soaked Dorian because I'd jump back out of the way. He took it all with a sense of humor and a lot of laughs. I could tell he was just glad to have Buffy back.

After we got Buffy out of the tub and Dorian was drying her with a hair dryer set on low, which she enjoyed much more than the bath, my phone rang. It was my dad.

"Hi, Dad. How's Laney?" I asked.

"She's good, but I think she's ready to come home," he said.

"Okay, I'm at Dorian's but I will head home now," I said.

"See you there, kiddo," he said.

"You got this?" I asked Dorian after hanging up with my dad.

"I do," he said.

With that, we said our goodbyes. I headed out of the house listening to Dorian sing to Buffy as he finished drying her off.

As soon as I pulled into the driveway at Hangman's House, Dad pulled in behind me. I got out of my car and stood next to his while he took Laney out of her car seat.

"Do you want to come in?" I asked as he handed Laney to me.

She reached out her hands and babbled, "Mama."

"That's how we knew she was ready to come home," Dad said. "Otherwise, I think Brighton would have tried to keep her overnight."

"Well, I'm glad she's back," I said. "You and Mom can take her whenever you want, though."

"That extends both ways, Kinsley. If you ever need us to watch her, we're always happy to have her. I doubt you even need to call before you come by. Either of us is almost always there," Dad said.

"Thanks, Dad. Give Mom love from Laney and me."

"Will do, kiddo. And no thanks on coming in. Mom's making tater tot casserole, and I want to get back. She'll eat the whole thing if I'm not there," Dad said with a loving chuckle.

It was true, though. Witches could put away some tater tot casserole. In fact, it was what I decided to make for dinner as well.

"What about you, baby girl? What would you like for dinner?" I asked as we walked up the front steps.

Meri was right on my heels, and he darted into the house when I opened the front door. I put Laney in the high chair in the kitchen, and he jumped into the chair that sat closest to her. He was very attentive, and I couldn't tell if he'd missed her or felt bad for going with me.

"How about blueberries and..." I looked through the jars of baby food. "How about blueberries and squash?"

Laney laughed.

"I'll take that as a yes. Maybe some of this turkey too for protein."

The baby food meats weirded me out a little. It was like meat pudding, and I'd seriously considered just having Laney be vegetarian until she was ready to eat non-pudding meat. Thorn wasn't having it, though. He said she needed to grow up big and strong. I knew she could grow up strong without the turkey pudding, but I'd let him have the win. Thorn took his job as Laney's father seriously, and I didn't want to constantly override him just because I was home with her more.

"Turkey?" I asked again and made the jar do a little dancy.

She laughed and clapped her hands. Laney was only five months old, so it caught me off guard when she clapped. It was the first time she'd done it, so I made the jar dance again. When she laughed and clapped again, it filled my heart with such joy.

"You got any of those jars of ham?" Meri asked.

"The baby food ham?" I asked.

"Yes, that one."

"I do," I said. "Laney doesn't really like the ham."

"Good," he returned. "I'll take three."

"As you wish," I said.

I put Laney's food into a divided plate and dumped Meri's into his favorite bowl. As usual, Laney devoured her food. When she was done, I dragged her playpen into the dining room and set it up. She could play in there while I cooked dinner, and I'd be able to keep an eye on her. Not that she would have gone anywhere if I'd put her on a blanket on the floor, but I always figured better safe than sorry. Plus, she often fell asleep after eating, and I didn't want to find her snoozing on the hard floor.

Once I had her in the playpen, she reached up to me and opened and closed her little fists. That meant she wanted a bottle of formula. So, I made one really quick, and by the time I had the hamburger cooking on the stove for the casserole, she was asleep.

Laney didn't sleep as much as she did when she was a newborn, but she still slept a lot. It almost felt like she was charging up for something. Or, that was just one of my weird post-pregnancy thoughts.

When the beef was cooked, I drained it and then layered it in the pan with cream of bacon soup, tater tots, and a thick coating of shredded cheddar cheese on top. Most people used cream of mushroom soup, but I preferred bacon. When in doubt, always choose bacon.

I was in the process of pulling the casserole out of the oven when Thorn came through the front door. He'd ended up putting in a full day of work, and I wondered when he'd get the chance to make up for it. With a new dead body, it wasn't like he'd just be able to move his day off to the next day.

"That smells good," Thorn called from the living room. "Tater tot casserole?"

"It is," I called back.

"Where's Laney? Is she still with your parents?"

"She's in here," I said. "She was asleep."

Thorn appeared in the dining room. "Oh, sorry," he said, but he his smile stretched from ear to ear.

Laney wasn't the least bit fussy about being woken from her nap. She sat up and stretched her arms out so Thorn could scoop her up, which he did immediately.

"Don't worry, mama. I got this," He said and gave her an Eskimo kiss.

"I'll get dinner plated up," I said. "Try to get her back to sleep. If not, she can just play in there while we eat."

"Yes, ma'am," Thorn said with a mock salute.

Dinner was quiet other than the sound of Laney quietly babbling and watching us eat. By the time we'd finished our food, she'd fallen asleep again.

Thorn looked troubled, and when I was clearing the dishes was the first time I noticed. "Are you all right?" I asked.

"Just worrying about the case," he said.

"Are you going to tell me?" I asked. "I mean, what part of it is bothering you?"

"I don't suppose you'd let it go if I told you not to worry about it?" he asked.

"I mean, I guess I could," I said.

Thorn let out a sigh. "I wouldn't expect you to, and besides, you're sort of involved."

"Oh, wait, I'm not a suspect, am I?" I asked as I put the dishes in the sink.

"I'll dry," Thorn said. "And then I need to get to bed. I've got an early meeting with the FBI."

"The FBI?" I asked.

"We don't have forensic confirmation yet, but we think we have an identity on the skeleton," Thorn said.

"Oh."

Laney fussed a little but rolled over and went back to sleep. I nearly told Thorn to forget about it because I didn't want to know, but I didn't.

"She was a possible missing teenage runaway," Thorn said. "She was a minor when she ran away from home, but she'd be eighteen now."

"How long ago did she turn eighteen?" I asked.

"About six months," Thorn said.

"So, she could have died before," I said.

"She was a kid either way," Thorn said. "Just because she crossed some magical legal line… she was still a kid."

"A teenage runaway," I said.

"She could have been…" Thorn trailed off and didn't finish his sentence.

At first I wasn't sure what he was so upset about, but then it dawned on me. He was thinking that she could have been…

"She could have been me," I said. "Thorn, I, like, ran away and went to college. I had a scholarship. It wasn't the same thing, right?"

"You assume too much," he said.

"I don't know what you mean," I responded.

"I can't get into this. We don't even know for sure if it's her," Thorn said. "I'm sorry. I need to go to bed."

I understood. Curiosity was burning in my chest and pricking at the back of my brain like an itch I couldn't scratch, but there was also the part of me that didn't want to be involved.

That night I dreamed of Samara and the ghost who had led us to the skeleton in Nora's basement. They were joined by a teenager who looked a lot like me, but she wasn't quite me.

The nightmare was interrupted by the sound of screaming. When the screaming stopped,

Laney started to cry. It was all followed by the thunder of Thorn running down the stairs.

I'd fallen asleep on the sofa again, and Laney had been snoozing in her playpen. I'd woken her from her slumber with my screaming.

It had been months since I'd had night terrors, and I'd thought it was over. Thorn picked Laney up and she immediately stopped crying. But she was peering at me with fat tears threatening to spill over from her glassy blue eyes.

"Are you all right?" Thorn asked. "Was it a nightmare?"

"So it was me screaming?" I tried to confirm.

"It was," he said and pressed the back of his hand to my forehead.

"What are you doing?" I asked.

"You're burning up," he said. "You've got a fever."

"That's impossible," I said.

But I had a splitting headache, and my body hurt almost as much. When I tried to stand up from the sofa, it felt like all of my limbs were made of lead.

"You're burning up," Thorn repeated. "You've got a fever, and from what I can feel, it's a doozy."

"I don't get sick," I said.

I'd never been sick in my life. I had no idea what to even do.

"Well, you are now," Thorn said. "Why don't you lie back down on the sofa. Laney's calm, so we'll get you some tea and medicine."

"Meri can heal me," I protested.

"I've been lying on you the entire time," Meri said, and then he sneezed so hard, he fell of the couch.

"Is the cat sick too?" Thorn asked.

"He can't be," I said. "He can't be killed."

"Doesn't mean he can't get sick," Thorn said.

"That's got to be impossible," I retorted. "Cats and humans can't get the same cold."

"Well, you're not just a human and he's not just a cat. I'd say there's no precedence for this," Thorn said. "Lie down and I'll get you some tea and Tylenol for the fever."

"Should I take my temperature?" I asked, remembering that's what people on television did when they got sick. "There's a thermometer in Laney's things. Someone gave us a kit as a gift."

Not all of my well-wishers after Laney was born were witches. I'd gotten some human-type gifts from people. They didn't know that witches can't get sick.

"Oh, no, the baby!" I exclaimed. "What if she gets this?"

"She seems fine," Thorn said. "Besides, babies get colds. It's not the end of the world."

It sure felt like it.

"You need to go back to bed," I said. "You've got that early meeting."

"Oh, sweetie. I'm up now," Thorn said with a chuckle. "That scream ensured that I won't be going back to sleep. I'll get you the tea and Tylenol. I've got to call Jeremy and see if he can handle the meeting with the FBI."

"You don't have to do that. I'll be all right. I feel like crap, but I think I can manage. The Tylenol will make the fever go away, right?"

"Yeah, it's pretty good at that," Thorn said.

"So some medicine and some matcha and yerba mate tea will fix me right up," I said. "Bacon for Meri."

"That will help considerably," Meri said.

"I'm going to call your mom then," Thorn said.

"No, you cannot have her come over here. If she gets sick..." I said. "I don't know what's going on, but I can't expose them anymore than I already have."

"I at least want her on standby, Kinsley. If I'm going to leave for work, I at least want to know you've got backup in case you get sicker," Thorn said.

"Okay," I relented. "But tell her not to come here. I will call her if I need her badly."

An hour later, Thorn was gone to work and my mom was on my front porch knocking. "Mom," I said as I opened the front door. "You didn't have to come here. You shouldn't have come here. I could get you sick."

She waved me off and stepped into the house. "Please, Kinsley. You constantly forget that I grew up in the human world. I didn't even come to Coventry until I was in my thirties. My powers had shriveled into nothingness before I got here. So, I've been sick before. I've got a fully functioning human immune system thanks to having colds, flu, chickenpox, and everything in between."

I looked at her horrified.

"Yeah, I had chickenpox."

"You don't think I have chickenpox, do you?" I asked.

Mom laughed. "No, sweetie," she said and put the back of her hand against my head. "What are your other symptoms?"

"I'm a little tired. More so than usual. My body sort of feels like concrete when I move my arms and legs. Oh, and a headache," I said.

"Where is the headache?" she asked.

"It's around here," I said and pointed to the sides of my nose, my eyes, and my eyebrows.

"That sounds like your sinuses. Anything else?" she asked.

"Meri sneezed," I said. "He seems to be sick too. Oh, and I woke up screaming and scared Laney."

"Any cough? What about your throat?" Mom asked.

"I haven't had a cough," I said. "There might be a tickle in the back of my throat now that I'm paying attention."

"Sounds like it's probably just a bad cold, but we'll keep an eye on it," Mom said.

"I really don't want you to get sick, Mom. Even if it's just a cold, I'm not sure if you should stay here and risk it," I said.

"Are you trying to tell me you don't want me here?" Mom asked, but her voice betrayed no emotion.

It wasn't a manipulation. She really wanted to know, and I was certain if I told her I'd rather be alone, she would have left with no hard feelings. But that wasn't the case at all. I really was just worried about her.

"No, Mom. I'm just worried about you. And dad too. All the Aunties. If I'm not protected, then you guys aren't either," I said.

"Well, I'm protected by a giant dose of elderberry, echinacea, and vitamin C I took before I came here," she said with a chuckle. "I've got some for you too. Oh, and I brought the stuff to make chicken soup," she said and patted her bag. "So, you and Meri settle in on the sofa to watch a movie, and I'll make soup."

There was no talking her out of it, so I gave her a hug and did what she said. It wasn't lost on me that she was getting the chance to be my mom again. I'd taken that from her when I left at seventeen. I thought I was a big-time adult making real grown-up decisions, but I'd bet she had a lot of years of mothering left in her.

And as much as I wouldn't want to admit it to myself, it felt good to have her there to take care of me. Although, after about another half an hour, the Tylenol had fully kicked in, and I felt a great deal better.

I wandered into the kitchen where she was ladling soup into one of my ceramic bowls. "Hey, you're supposed to be resting," Mom protested.

"I feel better," I said. "Thorn gave me tea and medicine before you got here, and I think it's kicking in."

"I'd feel better with some bacon," Meri said as he sashayed into the kitchen behind me.

"You feeling better, buddy?" I asked.

He scowled at me. "No, but like I said, bacon would help."

"I'll get it," I replied with a chuckle.

"No, I'll get it," Mom sidestepped and blocked my path to the fridge.

"Really, Mom. I'm feeling much better," I said.

"That's just because of the Tylenol, sweetie. You don't want to push yourself too hard because you're artificially feeling better," she said.

Just then, Laney started to fuss a little. "I'll change her," I said. "You can take care of Meri and get the soup ready. Do people even eat soup for breakfast?"

"I can make you something else," she said.

"That's not what I mean. Sorry I teased. It smells amazing," I said.

"Well, good. That means your head isn't all blocked up. The soup will help with that even more."

"Be right back," I said.

I picked Laney up from her playpen and took her to the changing table. After a fresh diaper and some new jammies, she was smiling and making a game of poking me in the cheek. I started making a fish face and blowing when she did it which made Laney cackle hysterically.

I was about to head back into the kitchen with her when someone knocked on the door. "Grand Central Station here today," I said.

Since I was already feeling so much better, I opened the door. I'd completely forgotten that I was terrified of getting everyone sick. Dorian stood on the other side of the threshold somehow looking both serious and excited.

"Dorian," I said. "Come in."

"Aren't you afraid you're going to give him the plague?" Mom called from the kitchen.

"Crap, right. Dorian, I'm sick," I said. "I've got a fever, and I woke up feeling like crap."

"Oh," he said and rubbed the back of his neck. "Is it serious?"

"Mom says it's probably just a cold, but maybe you shouldn't be here. I don't want to get you sick," I said.

"A cold?" he said with a laugh. "Jeez, Kinsley, your tone of voice made it sound like the plague had returned for real. It's fine. I've got an immune system of iron. I'm comfortable taking my chances."

"Well, we're about to have soup. Would you like to join us?" I asked.

"Sure," he said. "I came here to talk to you about some stuff. We can do that over soup. And coffee?"

"Coffee's just about done," Mom said as we walked into the kitchen. She got Dorian a bowl of soup and then took Laney from me. Mom put her in the highchair and then made her a bowl with just broth and some carrots. "I'll feed her once it's cooled enough."

I got Dorian and myself a cup of coffee, and we sat down at the table. "Wait, is this your first time being sick?" Dorian asked.

"How did you guess?" I asked.

"Well, I don't think I've ever seen such a production made over a cold," he said. "It's sweet," he said to my Mom.

"Witches don't usually get sick," I said. "At least not this close to the ley line."

"You haven't told me enough about what's going on with you," Dorian said. "Maybe we could discuss it on a little outing? You know, like we used to…"

"But I'm sick," I said.

"I know. I should have called or texted you first," Dorian replied. "I was just so excited that I headed over here right after Isaac left this morning. I dropped Buffy off with the neighbor that babysits her and drove straight here."

"Your neighbor babysits your dog?" I asked.

"She loves it," Dorian said.

"The neighbor or the dog?" Mom asked.

"Both," Dorian chuckled. "I hate just leaving Buffy alone in the house, and Mrs. Kennedy likes having a part-time dog. She says she's too old to have one all to herself, but getting to borrow one is the perfect arrangement."

"I am feeling better," I said. "What got you so excited that you rushed over here? Maybe I could use a little fresh air. I thought I read somewhere it was good for the immune system not to stay cooped up inside when you're sick."

Mom was giving me the eye, but she didn't come out and say anything. I knew that no matter how silly she thought I was being, she wouldn't pass up the chance to watch Laney. Plus, she was already at our house and had planned to stay all day. It was perfect. Other than the fever thing, but that was under control.

"So, I was listening to the police scanner yesterday, and they found the missing girl's campsite," Dorian said.

"What?"

"Well, I don't know for sure or not if it was hers. Nobody has even confirmed it's her yet, but there is an abandoned campsite," Dorian said.

"But, Dorian, that body was a skeleton. She had to have been dead for a while. Weeks under the best of circumstances, but probably more like months," I said. "How could a campsite still be there after all that time?"

"Well, it turns out that the guy that runs the campgrounds isn't a very good businessman. So, even though the rent on the campsite hadn't been paid for months, he hadn't done anything about it. She was renting a crappy site that nobody ever wanted, and the meager rent wasn't enough for him to haul his butt down there and do anything about it," Dorian said. "So, it's all just still sitting there."

"What is sitting there, though?" I asked. "If she was living in a tent, there can't be much left after all this time."

"That's the thing. It's a camper van. It's an RV. And it's just sitting there while your husband and Jeremy negotiate with the FBI over who gets jurisdiction," Dorian said.

"So, we'd need to go now," I said. "Before they work it out."

"Mom?" I wasn't sure what I was asking her. For permission to go? To watch Laney? For advice?

"Do you want the mom answer or the Brighton answer?" she asked. "Because as your mom, I'd tell you to go rest on the couch. As Brighton, I know exactly why you feel like you need to go."

"I don't need to go," I said. "I know that."

"Because Thorn and the FBI will solve the case," Mom said.

"They will," I said. "This one is right up their alley. It doesn't involve us."

"But doesn't it?" Mom asked.

"You sound like you're trying to talk me into it," I said with a chuckle.

"Because I know you're going to be absolutely miserable to be around today if you don't go," Mom said. "There's a supernatural element to this case, so it falls under the purview of the Coven. That's all the reason you need. If you want a reason."

"We'll go check out the RV," I said. "It couldn't hurt to go take a look."

"I just want to sleep," Meri said.

"It's okay. You can stay with Mom and Laney. I'll be all right," I said.

That was all it took. He jumped up onto the arm of the sofa and made himself comfortable. I asked Mom if she needed anything while I was out, and she said she'd call Dad if she did.

I took a bottle of Tylenol and a Thermos of soup with me. Mom said it was in case I started feeling poorly while we were out.

Chapter Six

Once we were in the car and on our way to the campgrounds, Dorian opened up a little. "I don't have any doubts that your husband is capable as sheriff, but I have my doubts that he'll be allowed to solve this case," he said.

"What? What do you mean?" I asked.

"The FBI is going to come in swinging their big… badges, and then drop the ball. I can almost feel it," Dorian said. "Once it gets out who she was, it's not going to be a priority."

"What do you mean, Dorian? You're being cryptic."

"Well, when I found out who she was, I started poking around her social media. More like her former friends' social media. It still amazes me what kids just put out on the internet, but I guess it makes sense when they are talking smack about a girl they didn't particularly like."

"I'm still not getting it," I said.

"All of her former friends were big into the church, but not like a regular church. One of those super strict ones that pretty much cuts themselves off from most of society," Dorian said.

"Except for to post all of someone's private business on the internet?" I said.

"Yeah," he answered. "Anyway, Alicia was gay. She ran away from home because her parents were trying to force her into a conversion therapy camp before she turned eighteen."

"Jeez," I said and let out a breath I didn't know I was holding. "Those still exist?"

"Anytime people get the chance to be awful, they take it," Dorian said.

"To their own kids?" I asked.

"Some of them... especially to their own kids," he replied.

The tone of his voice and the way Dorian's jaw clenched told me there was something personal in all of this.

"Do you want to talk about it?" I asked.

"Just a boy from when I was in high school," Dorian said. "My first boyfriend, I'd guess you'd say. Long before I met Isaac. His father was a preacher and his mother was a narcissistic nightmare. They put him in conversion therapy when he came out, and he didn't make it."

"Oh, I'm sorry," I said.

"He was the seventeenth boy to commit suicide there over the camp's thirty-year history. His death got the place shut down. So, at least there's that. I think it would help Joey to know that his death saved other kids, but I wish it wouldn't have taken that," Dorian said. "You okay? You look pale and kind of gray."

I pulled down the visor mirror and looked. He was right, but I felt okay. "I'm fine. Probably just dehydrated. I'll drink my soup, if you don't mind."

"Go ahead," Dorian said. "Anyway, I've been seeing him."

"You've been seeing Joey?" I asked and wiped a little dribble of chicken soup off of my chin with the back of my hand.

"Yeah, I've been seeing his ghost," Dorian said. "This is going to sound nuts, but it's how I knew to turn the police scanner on. I saw him standing by it."

"I thought you probably kept that thing on all of the time," I said.

"I used to, but sometimes it bothered Buffy. So, I had it unplugged. I was working on one of my fiction books, and I looked up to see Joey standing by the scanner. I felt this weird impulse to hug him. Maybe not weird. We never really got to say goodbye. Anyway, I got up and walked over there but he vanished. I plugged the scanner in, and that's when I learned the stuff about Alicia."

I would have talked to him about it more, but we arrived at the campground office. Dorian pulled into a parking spot, got out of the car, and consulted the map hanging on an old wooden sign.

"Got it," he said as he hurried back into the car. "I don't think anyone saw me."

"I wasn't aware this was a covert mission," I said.

"Of course it is. We don't want anyone to know we're here. Especially not the office, but I don't think there was anyone in there."

"You're right. I don't know what I was thinking," I said.

"You sure you're okay?" Dorian asked.

"I'm great," I said. "Feeling even better than when we left."

It took a few minutes to get to the campsite, and we rode in silence. I stared out the window, watching the trees go by, and Dorian focused on finding our destination.

When we got there, I understood why no one really wanted the campsite. It was one of the furthest from the main road, but it wasn't close to anything interesting. It literally felt like the forest swallowed you whole, and perhaps that's why Amelia wanted it.

"Where would she have gotten this RV?" I asked Dorian as we got out of the car.

"I don't know," he said. "I hope the answer is inside."

"Did they mention on the scanner if she stole it from her parents or something?" I asked.

"Nothing like that," he said. "They didn't say, but it's possible. Or she could have stolen it from someone else."

"I don't want to assume she was a thief," I decided out loud.

"True, but we have to consider all of the possibilities," Dorian returned.

"I'm sorry," I said.

"For what?"

"That something like this is happening so close to home," I said with a shrug. "I know it can't be easy."

"Well, I've got good friends and an amazing husband now, so it's going to be okay. But it won't be for Amelia, and maybe helping her find justice will help me work out some stuff in my head," Dorian said. "Should we go inside?"

I looked over at the RV. It was an older model, and you could tell that even before it sat out in the elements for months, it hadn't been in the best shape. It was also possibly a murder victim's last home. I was about to tell Dorian that we shouldn't go in. I didn't want to mess up a potential crime scene and prevent law enforcement from solving the crime.

But then I saw her. Standing off in the trees was the ghost of the young woman I'd seen in my dream just before I woke up screaming.

She waved at me. It was the kind of shy, timid wave you offer someone when you're not sure if they are a friend but you hope that they are. My stomach clenched. She looked like a girl on her first day at a new school.

Then the ghost froze as if she heard something I didn't hear. She slowly turned her head around to look over her shoulder, and I tried to follow her eyes. But I didn't see anything. When she turned back, the look of sheer terror on her face was enough to make me shudder. Then she vanished, and I couldn't stop shivering.

"Kinsley, are you okay?" Dorian reached out and grabbed my hand. "Oh, wow, you're burning up."

I kept shaking. I was so cold that I wasn't sure I'd ever feel warm again. "Is my fever back?" I asked, and I could swear my teeth chattered a bit.

"I'm pretty sure it is. I think we should go," Dorian said. "We need to get you home. This was a bad idea."

"It's not, and we're not leaving yet. We've come this far, and this is our only chance to look around. I'll be all right," I said. "Um, I could just take some more Tylenol."

"You can't," he said and shook his head. "You can only have that every eight hours. It's way too soon."

"What could it hurt?" I asked.

"Have you been living under a rock? It could destroy your liver. That stuff is safe as long as you don't take too much," he said.

"I've just never needed it," I said.

"You could take ibuprofen. Do you have any? It's okay for you to take both of them at the same time," Dorian said.

"I don't. I mean, I don't keep stuff like that in my purse. I've never needed it," I said.

"Wait, I have a bottle in my glove box. I keep some for Isaac. He gets migraines," Dorian said.

I stood studying the RV while Dorian grabbed the medicine from his car. When he returned, he handed me two small orange pills. I swallowed them and noticed a sharp stab in my throat.

"You winced," Dorian said.

"It hurt a little when I swallowed those," I said.

"Huh… Okay. Well, that could be a sore throat, or it could just be raw from your congestion," he said. "We should go home."

"Let's look around first," I said. "I took those pills. I'll take it easy, I swear."

He studied me for a moment, but I could see on his face how much Dorian wanted to go into the RV. We were tantalizingly close, and whether or not he felt a personal connection to the victim was irrelevant. Dorian was a reporter, and those instincts had already kicked in.

"All right, but if you start to feel like you can't handle this, you have to tell me," Dorian said.

"I will, I swear," I said.

We approached the RV, and Dorian went up the rickety metal steps to the door first. I'd wondered if it was unlocked, but Dorian was able to open the door easily. It hadn't even been latched all the way.

He opened the door and stepped inside. I stood on the last metal step and scanned the woods around us quickly before following him inside.

Other than the layer of dust on everything, it almost looked like someone had just stepped out. There was a half-full bottle of Coke on the dinette table and a book turned upside down to hold the page. I crossed the few feet between myself and the table and saw a small leather object on the bench.

"It's her purse," I said and picked it up.

Inside I found a wallet and confirmed the RV had been Alicia Holland's last home.

"Is that a driver's license?" Dorian asked as I studied her picture.

Her face was already familiar to me. I'd seen it in a dream and outside in the woods, and I'd known it was her before I knew.

"It is, and this was definitely Alicia's place," I said and handed Dorian the license.

While he looked it over, I continued searching her purse. It felt like a gross violation, but there was probably more information in her handbag than in the rest of the RV. We keep what is most precious to us close, so it meant that something significant had happened if Alicia left without her purse.

Besides the license, her walled contained a bus pass and three dollars. There was a picture of a blonde girl too tucked into the section under the license holder.

"You were on Alicia's social media, does this girl look familiar?" I asked and handed Dorian the picture.

He studied it for a moment. "She was in some pictures with Alicia. Arms around each other and smiling, but they weren't couple-type pictures. It was more in groups where everyone was doing the same things."

"Then it was a secret to more than just her parents," I said. "I would maybe think it was just a picture of a friend tucked in her wallet, but it's the only one."

"Yeah, and they obviously had more friends," Dorian said. "Both of them seemed popular. If you can judge that sort of thing from a picture, and most of the time you can..."

"You don't think this girl could have had something to do with it?" I asked. "Maybe jealousy or revenge for outing her? When Alicia's parents found out, it might have caused problems for this girl too. Especially if they were all involved with the same church."

"I'll get her name when I get home and look closer at her social media," Dorian said. "So what's the potential theory?"

"That Alicia invited this girl here to see her. Maybe she ran but missed her too much, so she found a way to contact her."

"And then the girlfriend killed her?" Dorian asked.

"Maybe. If it was revenge," I said with an uncertain shrug. "Perhaps they got into a fight, or it was an accident. Even if Alicia's death was an accident, this girl might have been scared to tell anyone. Simply being here might have been a huge risk."

"I'll find out who she is. Maybe we can call her or message her online," Dorian said. "She might talk to us if she doesn't have to be seen with us."

"I don't know if that will be necessary," I said. "I'm speculating pretty wildly here based off a photo in a wallet."

"A photo that was probably her significant other," Dorian said. "Isn't that where the cops look first?"

"It is, but… Do you still want to be involved if that's the case?" I asked.

"What do you mean?" Dorian asked.

"Well, you want to solve this case to get justice because Alicia is a gay teen runaway. What does it do to your motivation if it was her girlfriend who did it?"

113

Dorian opened his mouth to respond right away, and I wondered if I'd said something super offensive. Then, he closed it and rubbed his chin.

"I want to clear her then," he said. "Because if it gets out that these two were involved, and the cops look at the significant other first, they might destroy this girl too."

"That makes sense," I said. "And I'm sorry if I said something offensive."

"I'm gay, Kinsley. I'm not a delicate flower," Dorian said with a chuckle.

"I mean, you kinda are," I teased.

"Good that you still have your sense of humor," he said. "Let's look around and see what else we find."

But there wasn't much else in the RV. There were a few changes of clothes and very little food in the kitchen. She had a sketchbook full of drawings on her bed. I shouldn't have done it, but I picked it up and put it in my bag. I told myself that it probably wasn't evidence anyway, and Alicia wouldn't have wanted her parents to end up with it.

"I think I need to sit down," I said as I joined Dorian back out in the living room area.

I'd begun to feel a little lightheaded.

"Let's get you out to the car and back home. Your mother and husband will kill me if you get sicker. I never should have gone through with this," Dorian said.

"Yes, but we have a lead," I said as I swooned.

My hand shot out and grabbed the edge of the dinette table. It was then I realized that Dorian and I had left our fingerprints all over everything.

"Our fingerprints," I said.

"Well, we haven't touched much in here, and I've been wiping them off," Dorian said.

"I just hope we didn't wipe off the killer's," I said as he put his arm around me and guided me the couple of feet toward the camper door.

Just then, it flung open and banged against the wall. An angry-looking man stomped into the RV and glared at Dorian and me.

"Who are you?" he demanded. "What are you doing in here?"

"Who are you and what are you doing here?" I shot back without really thinking about it.

"Tell me who you are, or I'm calling the cops," the man said, but he made no move to take out his phone.

"We're hikers," Dorian said. "We happened by this campsite, and the RV door was open. We thought we heard someone call for help, so we came in. Sorry."

"Well, you guys have terrible timing," the man said and rubbed his stubbly jowl with his palm. "This is my campground. Burt Hodges is the name. Did you guys do anything in here? Did you steal anything?"

"Of course not," I said. "We just got here. There's no one in here, so we were on our way out."

Burt studied me for a moment before taking a look around. "You guys didn't touch nothin'?"

"No," Dorian said. "We really just thought someone was hurt in here. Must have been an animal or something nearby. You know how the forest distorts sounds."

Burt grunted at that, and I had my serious doubts he knew anything about the forest at

116

all. He didn't strike me as the outdoorsy type, and I wondered how he'd come to own a campground. I wasn't going to ask, though.

"Like I said, you guys have terrible timing. The cops and the FBI are on their way here. Hope you really didn't touch anything or your fingerprints might be on a crime scene," Burt said.

"We didn't. I promise," I lied.

"Well, get outta here," Burt said. "Unless you want to hang around and talk to them too."

"Thank you," Dorian said.

He grabbed my by the hand and pulled me out of the RV. We had to squeeze by Burt. He'd liberally applied Old Spice some time in recent history. I was congested and it still burned my nostrils. Even worse was that my illness and the potent aftershave didn't cover the lingering smell of stale beer clinging to Burt.

A violent shiver hit me when we stepped outside. Dorian put his arm around me again and led me to the car.

"I thought the ibuprofen was supposed to help," I croaked out.

At some point, my throat had become raw. It felt like gargling broken glass whenever I talked… or had to swallow.

I opened the passenger side of the car and plopped down inside. It felt good to sit down. I hadn't realized how much energy it'd been taking to stand until I was off my feet.

"You okay?" Dorian asked. "I know I keep asking that, but you sound terrible."

"My throat hurts," I said.

"Did it hurt before?" Dorian asked.

"A little, but nothing like this," I said. "No more talking."

"Okay," Dorian said and shut my door. He walked around the front of the car and got into the driver's side. "We should go to the store and get you some lozenges."

I nodded my head yes.

"Or, do you think your mom would make you something? Like a tea that would work better that store-bought medicine?"

"My store," I muttered out.

"You've got it," he said.

Chapter Seven

I fell asleep on the short drive from the campgrounds to my store. Dorian shook my shoulder gently when we got there.

"If you give me a list, I can get what you need. I'd hate for you to have to get out and walk around," he said.

"I need marshmallow root, licorice root, nettles… You know what, I'll come in," I said.

"Well, let me come around and help you," he said.

I was about to tell Dorian I wasn't feeling well, and that I was perfectly capable of getting out of the car on my own, but he was too fast. He was out and around on my side in a flash. Dorian offered me a hand.

I took it and he helped me to my feet. I wanted to make a joke about how people would gossip and then waggle my eyebrows, but I decided it wasn't worth the pain.

"I can feel the heat coming off of you," Dorian said as we made our way to the shop's door. "I no longer think there is any chance at all that this is a cold. We should get you to the doctor."

"Let me try the tea first," I said and winced.

"Kinsley, you are being unreasonable," Dorian said. "Completely unreasonable."

"Then I must be feeling like my old self," I said and opened the door to the shop.

As soon as I stepped inside, I felt a little better. I had no idea why, and it was all probably psychological, but being inside my store made me feel more alert. My throat hurt a bit less when I swallowed too.

"Kinsley!" Reggie said cheerfully. "What are you doing here? It's so good to see you."

"Stay back," Dorian warned. "She's got the plague, and she insists on making some sort of tea instead of going to the doctor. I've already been exposed, but you might want to stay back."

"I'm sorry," I said. "I didn't think about how sick I might make you."

"Yes, you have," Dorian reminded. "We went through all of that over an hour ago. I made the choice to spend time with you, and I've already been exposed to your plague germs. Don't fall apart on me now. Just point at the herbs you need, I'll take them up to the register, and we'll get you home."

"She does look terrible," Reggie said. "I didn't see it at first, but, man, Kinsley, are you sure you're okay?"

I nodded my head yes and walked over to the shelves lined with baskets of herbs. Dorian offered Reggie a shrug and followed along behind me. I picked out the things I needed and then went back to the car while Dorian checked out.

"You didn't need to pay," I said when he got back in the car.

"It wasn't expensive," he countered.

"That's not what I mean," I said. "Those were already my herbs. It's my shop."

"Oh, right," He said with a chuckle. "Well, actually buying them and all that makes it easier on Reggie. One less thing she'll have to rectify during inventory."

"Good call," I said.

And then I don't know what happened. The next thing I knew, I woke up to an annoying beep and the smell of antiseptic. I felt a sting in my arm and scratchy sheet on my back and legs.

The hospital.

"What?" I asked and tried to sit up too fast.

"Whoa, take it easy," Thorn's voice was calm and soothing.

I looked around and saw that I was in the hospital, but not a regular room. "I'm in the ER?" I asked. "Where's Laney?" Panic gripped my stomach, and I almost threw up.

"She's okay," Thorn said and took my hand. He was sitting on a stool next to the bed. "Don't know if Dorian is ever going to recover, but Laney is just fine. She's still with your Mom and Dad at the house."

"What happened? I was on my way home to make tea," I said.

"Well, Dorian thought you died. Like I said, I don't know if he's ever going to recover from the fright you gave him. He thought I was going to beat him to a pulp, but I know you," Thorn said and squeezed my hand. "How long did he try and talk you into going home and resting before you blacked out?"

"Quite a while," I said.

"I figured," Thorn said. "I heard a rumor that you guys were out snooping around an abandoned RV."

"Thorn, I'm sorry…" I started to say, but he cut me off.

"No, I don't want to know. Don't tell me anything that I might feel obligated to tell the FBI. As far as I'm concerned, for now, the two of you were out getting some air in the woods," Thorn said.

"So, what really happened to me?" I asked.

"You had a high fever and severe dehydration," Thorn said. "The IV is fluids and some antibiotics."

"Antibiotics?" I asked.

"Yep, the fever and dehydration were thanks to rip-roaring case of strep throat. Normally, they would just give you pills to take at home, but the doctor was worried about how bad your case is. Oh, they also gave you a shot of steroids in your butt. Your throat was swelling shut," Thorn said.

"I've heard of strep throat," I said. "I had no idea it was that bad."

"It's usually not," Thorn said. "But occasionally it gets out of control. Leave it to you to have the worst case the doctor has ever seen."

"Well, I mean, if you're going to do something, might as well give it your all," I said and laughed. "Hey, my throat doesn't hurt nearly as much."

"That's the steroids," Thorn said. "They're going to send you home with a prescription for ibuprofen too."

"I can get ibuprofen at the store," I said. "Dorian had some."

"These are prescription strength. They will keep the pain and inflammation away."

"I'm all for that," I said. "When can I leave? They're not admitting me, are they?"

"I don't think so," Thorn said. "Though I tried to convince the doctor he should."

"Thorn Wilson, you did not," I scolded.

"Just overnight for observation. I've never seen you get this sick before. I'm worried," he said.

"I'm feeling a ton better," I said and pushed myself up to sitting.

Thorn helps me adjust the back of the bed so I could still recline a little. "I'm glad," he said. "You look a lot better than when I got here."

"I'm going to choose not to take that as an insult," I said and pulled my hand away so I could cross my arms over my chest.

"That's my girl," he said. "Are you going to be mad at me if I step into the hall and call Jeremy? I need to fill him in on your condition. I know he's worried."

"Yeah, and I should call my Mom," I said.

"I'll call her too," he said. "You rest your throat."

"Really quick before you go... Where is Dorian?" I asked.

"He had to leave to go get the dog from the neighbor. He'll be back as soon as Isaac is off work. That should be any time now," Thorn said.

"Thanks. Love you," I replied.

"Love you too."

He stepped out into the hall to make his calls, and I began trying to figure out how to turn on the television. I was only messing around with it for a moment or two when Dorian came into the room.

Dorian rushed over to my bed and practically collapsed on top of me. "Oh, gawd, I'm so glad to see you alive."

I had to laugh even though he was completely serious. "People are going to talk if anyone comes into the room and sees you half on my bed and practically on top of me," I said, but I hugged him hard. Also, I was happy because I finally got to make my joke.

Dorian sat up and narrowed his eyes at me. "Well, I guess you're going to live," he said and stuck his tongue out at me.

"Unfortunately," I said with a heavy, dramatic sigh. "You can't get rid of me that easily."

"Oh, gawd, Kinsley. I almost let you die," he said.

"No, you didn't. I was just dehydrated and had a bit of a fever."

"A bit of a fever? Woman, they were talking about ice blankets and pumping you full of cold salt water. When I first brought you in, the doctors were talking like you might have septic shock. I thought you were going to die!" Dorian moaned.

"You mentioned that," I said and grabbed his hand. "It's okay, though. It's just a sore throat and apparently my body decided to be dramatic about it."

"I'm so glad you're okay. You're taking this so well. I'd be freaking out if I woke up in a hospital," Dorian said.

"Well, you're freaking out for both of us," I replied.

"You just scared me." Dorian's face relaxed a little. "Don't you ever do that to me again."

"I won't," I swore. "So, I guess I have to stay here until they are done topping off my fluids, but then I get to go home."

"They're not going to keep you for observation? A couple of hours ago, they thought you were dying."

"You thought I was dying," I corrected. "No, I'm not staying. Thorn tried to convince the doctor, but I'm going home later. Not being admitted."

"Well, what should we do while we wait?" Dorian asked.

"I'm not supposed to be talking this much," I said and felt my throat getting raw again.

"I'm going to go out there and get you some Sprite and a grape popsicle. I know those nurses keep some behind the counter. When I get back, we'll do some web sleuthing. Sound like a plan? Then you can point, and I can click."

I nodded my head yes.

Dorian left the room and was back in under five minutes. He had a cup of ice, a can of Sprite, and two grape popsicles. I watched as he pulled the bed table over, poured my drink, and unwrapped one of the popsicles. "The other ones for me," he said as he handed me the one he'd already opened.

"You deserve it," I said.

"Oh, honey, no. Don't think you're getting off the hook that easily. When you're better, you're taking me out for dinner and then appletinis. And you are paying. I saved your life," Dorian said before biting the end of his popsicle.

I just laughed and nodded my head yes again. He hadn't actually saved my life, but dinner

and appletinis with Dorian sounded good to
me.

Dorian pulled the stool up as close to the bed as he could get it and angled himself so that I could see the screen. He brought up a social media site I wasn't too familiar with and said, "This is the one all the kids are using now."

"I'm not familiar with it," I admitted.

"That's because you're still using all the old lady sites," he teased.

"I'm not that much older than you," I snarked back.

"Still…" he said and began typing again. "So, I was thinking about something."

"Oh, no," I said.

"Hush. I was going to say something in the car, but then you passed out. Anyway, I was thinking about that Burt guy. Isn't it weird how he paid no attention to Alicia's missed rent and RV until the morning the authorities were supposed to search it? What was he doing there when he caught us? Because we were trying to figure out who killed her, but I'm sure that's not what he wanted."

"You're right," I said. "Do you think he was trying to hide something?"

"I'll bet that's what it was," Dorian said.

"So, then we don't need to go through the girlfriend's social media? You think it was Burt. Should we focus on him?" I asked.

"We should still look," Dorian said. "I don't have definitive proof it was Burt, so we need to keep all the lines of investigation open."

Before I could answer, Thorn came into the room. "I need to go meet with the FBI," he said. "They are hauling the victim's RV away, and they want local representation available. I told them I'd send Jeremy, but my contact was insistent that I at least make an appearance."

"Did you tell them your wife is in the hospital?" Dorian asked, and Thorn looked taken aback.

"I did," Thorn said. "Which is why I am going to call my contact's boss and tell them we can arrange another time to meet and that Jeremy can be there when they take the RV."

"No," I said. "Don't do that. I've got Dorian here."

"I'll just go make an appearance, and I'll be right back," Thorn said.

"You don't have to do that," I insisted. "This is my fault for pushing myself too hard when I should have known better. But that doesn't matter. I feel so much better. The fluids and steroids must be doing their thing because I barely even feel like I've got a cold. My fever's got to be way down."

"If I let myself get involved, I could get stuck there for a while," Thorn said.

"Dorian can take me home," I replied.

"Yeah, I can do that. When they discharge her, I've got no problem giving her a ride," Dorian said.

"Nowhere but home," Thorn said to Dorian pointedly. "If I find out you dragged her into the woods again, I will arrest you for something." And then Thorn turned to me. "And I'll arrest you too. Take care of yourself."

"How's Laney? She's not getting sick, is she?" I asked.

"Your mom says she's just fine. She and your dad want to take Laney overnight to give your antibiotics twenty-four hours. I told them you would let them know when you got home," Thorn said.

"That's how long I'll be contagious?" I asked.

"It is," Dorian said and patted my hand.

"You go," I said to Thorn. "Dorian and I will work all of this out."

"Take good care of her," my husband said to Dorian.

He kissed me and then left.

"Okay, so this is the girlfriend, I think," Dorian said and turned the laptop screen a little more toward me. "It looks like her, right?"

"Camilla Page," I said. "Yeah, that's her."

"You just relax and let me go through her stuff. I scratched the surface already, but I wanted your confirmation it was her before I dove too deep," Dorian said.

I plucked at the blanket over my legs and stared at the wall while I drank my Sprite. We'd already long since finished our popsicles, and I was starting to get hungry. I took that as a good sign. "You don't get a meal in the ER, do you?" I asked Dorian.

"You want me to get you something to eat?" Dorian asked. "I can go down to the cafeteria."

"Is that allowed?" I asked.

"As me if I care," he returned.

"I should wait for the doctor to tell me it's okay for me to eat," I said.

"Have it your way," Dorian said.

He went back to clicking away. I was about to pick up the television remote and start trying to work it again when Dorian turned and looked at me with wide eyes. "What? What is it?" I asked.

"There's another girl," Dorian said. "I mean, there was a new girl in the group."

"Oh?" I asked.

"Around the time that Alicia ran away, a new girl starts appearing in all of the pictures with the others. I didn't notice the shift until now, but looking at Camilla's pictures after Alicia was gone, there are a lot of the new girl. More of just the two of them than of the entire group together. It would appear that after Alicia ran away, Camilla and this new girl started spending a lot of time together."

"But if Alicia was gone and out of the picture, there wouldn't have been any reason for either of them to hurt her," I said. "What do you think it means? Because you've still got this look on your face."

"I don't know what it means," Dorian said. "But I'm not convinced that it means nothing."

Chapter Eight

Two boring hours later, I was released from the hospital. Thorn was still gone, so Dorian helped me out to his car.

"I want to stop for something to eat," I said as Dorian helped me into his passenger seat. I felt like a little old lady with him fussing over me.

"Your husband said he'd arrest me if I took you anywhere but home," Dorian countered. "And I believe him. We can order delivery when we get there."

"Delivery will take like a half hour," I complained.

"You have snacks at the house. Don't try to play me, Kinsley. I know you keep lots of snacks," Dorian chastised.

"Fine," I relented. "Fine."

Dorian laughed as he closed my door and rushed around to the driver's side. I tried the entire way back to Hangman's House to get him to stop at every restaurant we passed. There were only a few, but he seemed ready to strangle me as we drove past the last one.

"You suck and I hate you," I declared.

"No, you don't," Dorian said as we turned onto my street.

"You're right, but you've got to make it up to me. Can you order sausage pizza, breadsticks, toasted ravioli, those mozzarella cheese sticks, tiramisu, and the chocolate chip cannoli?"

"Do you want the cheese-toasted raviolis or the ones with meat?" Dorian asked.

"Get both," I said as we pulled into the driveway.

"Anything else?" Dorian asked with a chuckle.

"If you want anything… I'm buying so get whatever you want," I said.

"Wait, that's all for you? You're not going to share?"

"I mean, if you want the same things, just double the order. If we have extra, it's all good reheated," I said. "Plus, Thorn will be home at some point. He doesn't eat as much as me, but who knows if he's eaten today," I said and pulled my debit card out of my purse. "Here, use this to pay for it all. Make sure you leave a good tip."

"All right," Dorian said as he took the card. Some people never got used to how much witches could eat.

We went inside the house, and Dorian went right to the dining room to set up his laptop. My mom was walking around rocking Laney and singing while Dad sat on the sofa petting Meri.

"How's he doing?" I asked Dad. I probably should have asked about Laney first, but Thorn had already told me she was okay. Plus, the smile on my Mom's face revealed that they were just fine.

"I'm feeling much better," Meri answered. "And I'm also right here."

"Sorry," I said. "I thought you might be sleeping. Your eyes were closed, but you're right... I won't ever inquire as to your health again."

"Whatever," Meri said and jumped off the sofa. "Thanks for everything," he said to my parents.

Dad got off the sofa as Meri ran upstairs. "I just fed him salmon and some bacon. Whatever was wrong with him must be tied to you somehow. He got pretty bad there for a while, but as soon as you were in the hospital, he started to get better."

"I'm so sorry, you guys," I said. "Thank you so much for watching Laney."

"You don't need to be sorry," Dad said. "We will take Laney anytime you want. You don't need a reason, and you don't need to feel bad about needing to get out of the house and spend time with your friend."

"I still think it's a good idea for you to let us take her with us," Mom said. "Just to keep her from getting sick. If you can't handle her being away or she can't, we can always bring her back. Any time of night, you know we'll drive her right back over here."

"I think it's a good idea," I admitted. I knew that a lot of the reason I'd gotten as sick as I had was my own doing, but I still didn't want to risk Laney getting that sick. "I took my first dose of the antibiotics at the hospital. Fortunately, you can fill your prescriptions there. I'll make sure I get three doses in twenty-four hours."

"Your father and I will be back here and on your porch twenty-four hours from your first dose," Mom said. "We promise."

Laney was asleep in my Mom's arms, and as much as I wanted to hold her and snuggle, I let them leave quietly. "Call me right away if she gets sick," I said.

The said they would, and then were gone. Dorian emerged from the dining room.

"Pizza and all the other stuff will be here in twenty minutes," Dorian said. "Don't kill me when you see your bank statement."

"I wouldn't," I said. "I'm the one who told you to order all that."

"Are you okay?" Dorian asked. "Is this your first time with the baby away?"

"It is, but I'm okay. She loves my parents, and I doubt it will upset her," I said. "Am I a bad mom for not falling apart?"

"Not at all. You've been doing nothing but Mom duty for five months. It's okay to take some time and breathe," he said.

"I'm sorry..." I started to say.

"Don't you dare apologize for focusing on your baby," Dorian cut me off. "Everyone understands. Everyone but you."

"Sometimes I feel like I'm doing everything wrong," I said.

"You're not, but it's absolutely normal to feel that way," Dorian countered. "You want to sit in the dining room or in here? I can bring the laptop into the living room."

"To eat?" I asked.

"No, to talk to Camilla. I reached out to her on the site, and she's going to chat with us. She's waiting for her parents to leave for some church thing," he said.

"Does she know why we want to talk to her?" I asked.

"Yes."

"And she's still willing?"

"I think she wants to know more about what happened to Alicia," Dorian said.

"Are you sure we should be doing this?" I asked.

"No, but when has that ever stopped us? Camilla is eighteen. Her parents might not like it, but she's free to talk to us if she wants," Dorian countered.

"Okay," I said. "But you're taking the lead on this."

"I planned on it," Dorian said.

"Are you doing a type chat or video?" I asked.

"Video," Dorian said. "And, I'm going to be recording it so we can go back later an analyze her responses if we want."

"Let's do it in here, then. That way I can sit next to you on the sofa, and she won't know I'm here."

"Yes, ma'am."

I got Dorian and myself a Coke from the kitchen and then snuggled up under a blanket on the opposite end of the sofa from him. I was about to ask him what we were going to do if the pizza arrived while he was chatting with Camilla, but a young woman's voice came through the computer.

"Hello? Are you there?" she asked.

"I am," Dorian said and plopped down on the sofa in front of the laptop. "Sorry, I was grabbing a drink."

"Okay. Hello," Camilla said. "We're going to have to make this quick. My brother is going to be home from practice soon, and he'll be nosy if he hears me talking to someone."

"Understood," Dorian said.

"So, I heard on the news that they found Alicia's body," Camilla said softly. "Do you know how she died?"

"How did you hear that on the news?" Dorian asked her. "As far as I know, the whole thing has been pretty quiet. We haven't had any major news outlets show up. Not that they ever do around here."

"I follow some small, independent news sources," Camilla said. "They write or vlog about cases that the national news doesn't care about. But I think that might change."

"What do you mean?" he asked.

"They might get interested. A gay teen runaway found buried in a new construction house? That's got sensational written all over it. I'm actually kind of surprised they haven't jumped on it yet, but no one in Alicia's family is talking either."

"Because of the church?" Dorian asked.

"If you want to call it that," Camilla retorted.

"What would you call it?" he followed up.

"What everyone else does. It's a cult. They're a Christian sect, though, so folks aren't so quick to make a huge deal out of it, but I'm getting out of here as soon as I can. I would've already left except... except for my brother. I'm staying until I can take him with me."

I got the feeling she wasn't talking about her brother. I poked Dorian in the leg and hoped he'd picked up on it too. He gave me an almost imperceptible nod.

"Does you brother want to leave?" Dorian asked. "How old is he?"

"He's sixteen, and he'll be graduating in a little over a year. Normally, we wouldn't be allowed to go to secular school, but the small town we live in is almost all church members. All the kids in school are in the church too, and so are most of the teachers. The ones that aren't respect it enough that it doesn't bother the Elders. Anyway, the parents let the kids go to school so they can play sports on the state's dime."

"Your brother's practice," Dorian observed. "Were you in sports?"

"Alicia and I both played basketball," Camilla said. "My new… I have friends that play volleyball."

"Your new what?" Dorian asked as gently as he could. She'd dropped a nugget of the story just then, and he would latch onto it like a pit bull. I only hoped that he could be delicate enough to keep her on the chat. If he got too aggressive, she could just log off, but Dorian was a professional. So, I took a deep breath and listened.

"I… I shouldn't talk about that," Camilla said.

"Why not?" Dorian returned. He'd do that. He'd keep answering her with questions until she either came clean or let something else slip.

"It feels wrong after finding out about Alicia," Camilla said. "I mean, I've felt guilty about it for so long. Mostly because I've always thought that Alicia was still alive. I thought she'd come back someday, and it would be a mess."

"What would be a mess?" Dorian asked.

"Just before Alicia ran away, a new family moved to town. They joined the church, and they have a daughter. She's a grade behind me, so I have to wait. Even if my brother won't go, we're leaving," Camilla said almost breathlessly. "Even if Alicia had come back, I wouldn't have gotten back together with her. Don't get me wrong, I loved… love her. But it was as a friend."

"Why's that?" Dorian asked. "Did you guys have a falling out?"

"It wasn't anything like that. Not for me anyway. We were only together because we were the only ones. The only gay girls here. She would have been my best friend for life, but I wasn't in love with her," Camilla said.

"Did Alicia know that?" Dorian's voice was so soft when he asked. He sounded like he was trying to coax a frightened kitten out of danger.

"Are you trying to imply that I'm the reason why she ran away?" Camilla's face turned bright red. "Well, I'm not. Her parents were going to send her to that awful place. Our breakup is the reason they found out. She was upset, and Alicia got sloppy. We've worked so hard to keep it all a secret, but we were outside fighting. Well, she was mad at me. We though we were far enough away from the house so her parents wouldn't hear us talking, but Alicia kept raising her voice. They heard her, and they knew. They knew when they saw me. Saw that she was yelling the things she was yelling at a girl. My back was turned, so her father didn't see my face. He came out expecting to find her arguing with a boy, but it was me. I heard him behind us, and I ran. I ran without looking back, so nobody knows it was me."

"You took a big risk talking to me," Dorian said.

"Like I said, Alicia was my best friend. She was my first love even if it didn't work out to be forever. I was hoping you could tell me more about how she died. Whether she was in pain or not. Maybe you could tell me if I… If I caused her to do this to herself," Camilla choked up at that.

Tears flowed down her face, and she tried to grind them away with the backs of her hands. I even heard Dorian sniffle for a second, but he composed himself in a flash.

"I don't think I should tell you too much about the investigation because it might prevent her death from being solved," Dorian said. "But I seriously doubt she killed herself."

"She was found buried, right? And there was... there wasn't much left?" Camilla swallowed hard.

Clearly someone had been talking, but who that could be was a mystery too big and not important enough to worry about. Focusing on small-town gossip about the murder would only distract us, and probably not lead us to the killer in any way.

"There isn't any evidence that I know of that Alicia committed suicide," Dorian said.

I watched as Camilla took a deep, shuddering breath. She seemed to relax, and when she wiped her tears away, no more fell.

"I should go soon," Camilla said. "My brother is going to be home any minute, and I need to get his dinner ready. He'll be starving."

"One more question," Dorian started. "Do you think it's possible that either of Alicia's parents could have had anything to do with her death?"

"I have to go, my brother just walked in," Camilla said and disconnected the chat.

The thing was, I hadn't heard anyone. If her brother had arrived loudly enough for her to hear, there was a good chance Dorian and I would have heard it too. It was almost as if Camilla hadn't wanted to answer the question about Alicia's parents. She had wanted to avoid it so much that she cut the chat and never gave Dorian a chance to answer her questions. Because other than stating he didn't believe it was suicide, he'd skirted the rest of her questions.

"That was weird," I said as Dorian closed the laptop.

"You don't think her brother really got home?" Dorian asked.

"I don't know," I said. "Let's find a movie to watch. I just want to rest and eat my weight in junk food. I don't want to think about a parent hunting down their child and killing them for being gay anymore today."

But there was no way I was going to be able to stop thinking about it… or the look in Camilla's eyes just before she switched off the chat.

Chapter Nine

The next morning, I slept in about an hour. I panicked for a second because I could feel that Laney wasn't in the house with me, but I quickly remembered she was with my mom and dad.

I sent Dad a text asking him how she was doing and how their night had gone. He reported back that everything was great. Mom was in the kitchen fixing breakfast, and Laney was in the playpen watching. He was getting ready to take her out for a walk in the stroller.

"Do you need me to bring her home?" Dad asked earnestly.

"No, if she's okay, I'm okay. I'll see her at dinner," I said. "I'd ask you to put her on the phone, but I don't want to upset or confuse her."

"I'll call you right away if there are any issues, sweetie, but Laney isn't sick and she's having a good time with us," Dad said.

"I'm glad," I returned. "See you at dinner."

"See you then, pumpkin."

Thorn had already gone to work. He'd been more than happy to sit on the sofa watching a movie and devouring pizza with Dorian and me the night before. It had been weird not having the baby around, but it was also good to spend an evening with my husband and one of my best friends.

Since Thorn was gone, Dorian was probably furiously writing, and I had a day to myself, I decided to go see another friend. It had been a long time since I'd stopped into the Brew Station for a coffee and one of Viv's famous breakfast sandwiches.

I figured I could have a leisurely breakfast at the coffee house and then take food and a latte over to Reggie. She and a distant relative of mine named Eldridge were working. At some point, I'd need to get back to working in the shop and get a grasp on all of Reggie's new hires.

Once tourism opened in Coventry again, the town had been flooded with travelers and sightseers. Lots of ghost hunters and witches from around the country had begun spending time around town too, and that meant my shop had seen a boom in business. Reggie had needed to hire additional staff and I wasn't 100 percent familiar with all of them yet.

I went to my closet and grabbed a pair of black jeans and a heather gray sweatshirt. As I was putting my hair up in a bun, I noticed that streaks of black had begun snaking their way through my bright red tresses. It had been a long time since magic had made my hair color shift. I took it as a good sign.

What wasn't necessarily a good omen was that my eyes were turning black too. They'd looked a great deal more normal the day before, but as I gazed into the mirror, I saw that my irises nearly perfectly blended in with my pupils.

"Less dark magic," I whispered to myself. "I'll cut back."

As I turned from the mirror, it flickered. My imaged changed right before my eyes. The version of Kinsley reflected back at me no longer had black irises, but instead, my entire eye had turned black. The hair that had moments before been fiery red was completely black, but not in a good way. It was lifeless, and clumps had fallen out all over my head.

The reflection bared its teeth at me, and the ones that were still in my head had turned various shades of gray and brown. Most of them were missing, though.

I won't describe my skin other than to say I looked diseased, but more like I'd died from something awful.

"Kinsley!" Meri's voice startled me.

"You scared me," I said, and when I looked in the mirror, it was just regular old me. Well, mostly. The black streaks were still in my hair, and my eyes remained darkened.

"You were gripping the sink and shaking," he said.

"I'm fine," I said. "I just had a bad vision. I need to cut back on the dark magic."

"I'd say so," Meri said.

"Did you see it too?"

"No, but I can see it in you now," he replied.

"What do you mean?"

"Don't play dumb, Kinsley. It's the hair and the eyes," Meri snarked.

"My hair and my eyes have turned dark before," I said. "Right before my near-wedding to Thorn. Remember? It's not a big deal."

"That was different. Sure, they were black, but not like this. You have this dullness to you now," Meri said. "Almost a deadness."

"You're just being a jerk," I said.

"Whatever," Meri said, but when he turned to leave, his eyes lingered on me sadly for a few moments. "Stop being stupid."

"Whatever," I whispered back, but the look in his eyes was like a dagger to my heart.

Doesn't matter, I told myself as I put my shoes on and grabbed my purse. My hair changing told me that magic was coming back. Whatever had happened to it was reversing all on its own, and I wouldn't need to use dark magic anymore.

For anything.

That glimpse of myself in the mirror decaying from using black magic had really put the fear into me. I'd wanted a life without magic before, so I could accept living a life using very little of it now. I could not let myself become what I'd seen in my vision. I'd be no mother to Laney if it got that far.

I drove to the town square and parked my car outside of the Brew Station. A bunch of tourists were gathered near the statue in the middle listening to a guide tell the story of my family.

When I got out of the car, I felt a little tingle of something coming from the ley line that ran under the statue. I wanted to walk over and see if my magic was boosted by standing on it, but it was broad daylight and there were a ton of tourists around.

So instead, I headed into the coffee shop. Despite the huge feast from the night before, I was starving and more than ready for a hearty breakfast.

The morning rush was still in full swing, so I got in line and waited. At least the line wasn't out the door, but I was sure it probably had been less than an hour before.

Viv's face lit up when she saw me come in, and when Isaac came out of the kitchen to restock some of the hot items, he offered me a wave. The line moved quickly, and my stomach growled as I watched people walk over to tables with trays full of bacon, egg and cheese sandwiches, hash browns, and mountains of biscuits and gravy.

"What'll it be, love?" Viv asked when I got my turn at the counter.

"Biscuits and gravy, a bacon, egg and cheese biscuit, and a side of extra gravy," I said. "Oh, and a large hazelnut latte."

"You going to stick around?" Viv asked.

"Yes, I'm going to eat here," I said. "Laney is with my Mom and Dad, so I've got a day off."

"That sounds fun," Viv said. "Though I can't wait to see her again."

"I should bring her in more often," I said. "She'd probably love to be out and about, and I'd love more lattes."

"Speaking of that, let me get your breakfast and make your coffee," Viv said.

Some of the patrons in the coffee house were a bit horrified when they saw the food on my tray and realized it was all for me, but I didn't care. My favorite seat by the window was open, so I took it and watched the tour group until they disappeared into the courthouse.

I shifted in my chair, and when I did, I knocked my bag over. The sketchbook I'd taken from Alicia's RV came sliding out. I'd nearly forgotten I had it.

Since I still had more than half a latte and plenty of time, I decided to take it out and have a look.

The pictures weren't what I expected. I wasn't sure what I expected, but the drawings weren't it.

Alicia had been very interested in space. Many of the pictures were drawings of a night sky. There were also quite a few of planets. Some of them were of the planets in our solar system, but about halfway through, they appeared to be from her imagination.

The one I'd been staring at for five minutes was a lime-green gas giant surrounded by a pink series of rings. I was transfixed, but I eventually wanted to see what was next.

When I turned the page, a small slip of paper fluttered out and drifted to the floor. I leaned over and plucked it from the floor where one corner had wedged under my shoe.

The paper was a library receipt. It was a book about the space station on the Moon. The one we were going to use to launch commercial space flights to Mars. The space station on the moon, not the book.

I was getting ready to tuck the library receipt back into the notebook when an idea dawned on me. I hadn't seen the book in the RV, and I suddenly had a burning desire to find out if she'd returned it.

The status of her library book probably wasn't the most important piece of information in solving her murder, but I hoped it would lead me somewhere. I wasn't particularly fond of the idea of confronting Alicia's parents.

I told myself I would if I needed to, but I wanted to check the library first. "Hey, Viv, can I get a latte to go?" I asked as I stood up and tucked the sketchbook back into my purse.

"You got it," she said cheerfully.

A few minutes later, I had a latte in hand and was headed across the square to the library. I ignored the "no food or drinks" sign on the door as I pushed it open.

The woman behind the check-out desk eyed my coffee with disdain, but she didn't say anything. "Excuse me, I was looking for information on a book," I said.

"Could you step down to the information counter?" she asked. "This counter is for checking books out."

"Oh, sorry. I want information on a book's borrow history," I said. "I was hoping you could help me with that."

"I can't give you patron information," she said.

"But can you tell me if a book was returned?" I asked.

"I suppose I can do that," the woman huffed.

I handed her the library receipt. "I just want to know if my friend returned this book when she borrowed it. If not, I'll pay to replace it."

"Oh, well then. We always appreciate when people help the library," the woman said as she took the receipt.

I knew right then she wasn't a witch. The woman probably wasn't even aware the library had an entire other wing. It was split into two, after all. One side was just a regular library, and the other was filled with arcane and occult knowledge. It was for witches only.

My Great-Grandmother Amelda had run the library for decades, but she had recently retired. Now, the arcane side of the library was closed off except for by appointment only, and the public library was run by a regular librarian. Thanks to the internet, neither side was in as high demand as they once had been. Very few patrons milled around as the woman looked up the information on the slip I'd handed her.

"When this receipt was issued, the book was returned," the woman said. "Unfortunately, a later borrower did not, but you said you'd pay if your friend didn't return it. She did."

"I'll pay for a new copy anyway," I said and took out my debit card. "It seems like a popular book. I'd hate for others to miss out."

"Oh, that's so kind of you," the woman, her name tag said Patty, finally offered me a genuine smile. She ran the card and handed it back to me before typing a few things into her computer. "There we go. It's all ordered. Would you like an alert when it arrives so you can borrow it?"

"No, thank you," I said. "But could you tell me who checked it out and didn't return it?"

Patty's eyes narrowed. It didn't take much for her to catch on that I'd purchased a new copy in the hopes she'd give me information.

"I absolutely cannot do that. We cannot divulge our patrons' private information," she said.

"But you know who it was? Please make an exception this one time. The person who didn't return that book could very well be a killer," I said a little too dramatically.

"So you're with the police?" Patty asked skeptically. "Then you won't have any problem getting a warrant for the information."

People who worked in libraries were too smart for their own good. Patty gave me a look that told me to back off and have a nice day all at the same time.

"Thank you," I said and left the counter. I didn't want her calling Thorn. That would have been awkward and embarrassing. Getting arrested for harassing the library checkout lady wasn't on my to-do list for the day.

I had a choice. I could go home, watch movies, and eat leftover pizza until it was time for Laney to come home, or I could keep digging into Alicia's death. So, I got in my car and headed out of Coventry.

Chapter Ten

I'd taken my antibiotics, steroids, and a couple of Tylenols with my breakfast. By the time I got to the campground, I was feeling rather good. My spirits lifted even more when I saw a beat-up Toyota parked out in front of the offices. I'd driven out there with the hopes of talking with the manager, and it looked like he was actually there.

A dirty, sun-bleached "OPEN" sign hung in an equally dirty window. The pathetic clack of dusty, ancient bells sounded my entrance.

"We're full," Burt said as he appeared from a back room. "Oh, it's you," he said after a moment. "What do you want?"

"I want to talk to you about Alicia," I said. "Why were you in her RV the other day?"

"Why were you there?" he countered. "You know, I can still tell the FBI that I found some people nosing around in there. I'm sure they would love to talk to you."

"You're deflecting," I said. "You can call the FBI. I've got nothing to hide, and I had nothing to do with Alicia's death. Can you say the same thing? Because from what I've heard, you didn't care one bit about that RV until the FBI was coming to search it. You had zero concern that a young woman wasn't paying her rent on the campsite until you knew law enforcement was coming. Why is that, Burt?"

"She paid several months up front," Burt said. "I had no reason to be concerned until the sheriff contacted me. Not that it's any of your business."

"Where did she get the money to do that?" I wondered aloud.

Of course, Burt thought I was asking him. "I have no idea, nor would I care. People pay to rent a campsite, and I take the money. It's a fairly simple business, and I don't make it a habit to get into anyone's personal life. Most people are here for a week at most."

"So, did you think it was weird that she was here longer?" I asked.

"No, it happens. People have an RV and nowhere else to live. Can't afford the trailer park, so they live in the woods. The campsites have water, electric, and sewer hookups. As long as the person isn't consuming huge amounts of utilities, it's all included. Alicia got a deal because she wanted that site tucked away from everything. Nobody likes that one, so I have a hard time renting it. It was like she'd done me a favor," Burt said.

"Did you know she was underage when she first stayed here?" I asked.

Burt's face went a little pale. "Look, I already answered to the FBI about that. I rent campsites. I don't ask people for ID. She looked old enough, and she had an RV. I never would have suspected a seventeen-year-old would own an RV, so I assumed she was early twenties. I'm so old, it's hard to tell."

"This is probably a stupid question, but do you know where she got the RV? It wasn't her parents'," I said.

"Not a clue, but I feel like the FBI is really interested in that since they hauled it off," Burt said. "Look, I went into the RV that day because I was curious. I know that sounds ghoulish, but it was a kind of a big deal. You watch all those murder mystery documentaries on Netflix, and it was happening right here in my campground. I wanted to get a look inside in case, you know…"

"Netflix ever called?" I asked.

"Yeah, so what? There wasn't anything hinky going on with me and the girl, if that's what you're after," Burt said.

"Why would you think that?" I asked.

"Duh, because I've seen every true crime docuseries on Netflix," Burt said. "The girl was nice, though. Mostly kept to herself, but if I was ever in the office, she'd come in and borrow a book." He waved toward a dilapidated bookshelf behind him. I hadn't noticed it until just then.

Most of the books were shelved vertically, but a few had been stuck haphazardly in front of them horizontally. One of them was extraordinarily familiar, and my heart jumped into my throat when I realized why.

"It was you," I said and backed toward the door.

"What?" Burt looked confused, and at the same time, he took a step back toward the doorway he'd come from before.

"That book," I said and pointed at the same book I'd found the library receipt for in Alicia's sketchbook. "Alicia checked that book out from the library, and the next person never returned it. Were you…. Were you stalking her?"

I couldn't quite put the pieces together in my head, but I knew it meant something. I just knew it couldn't be a coincidence.

"This book?" Burt asked as he picked up the one.

I was already to the door. My hands were behind my back and ready to push my way out into the open if he lunged at me.

"Yes," I said. "Were you obsessed with her or something?"

"It wasn't anything like that," he said. "Look." Burt opened the book and showed me the inside of the cover. "It's not a library copy. This is my book. Alicia borrowed it from me, and I let her keep it. Eventually, she went into town and checked it out from the library. When she did, she brought mine back."

"Why would she do that?" I asked. "Why would she get it from the library if you let her borrow it for as long as she wanted? That doesn't make any sense."

"I don't know," Burt said. "It's just a book. I don't remember…"

Was he lying? I didn't entirely trust him, but I hadn't run out the door either. When he spoke again, I was glad I didn't.

"Wait, I remember now. There was another camper who wanted to read the book. She checked it out from the library so her friend could borrow mine. Alicia brought it back to me and said another friend was interested in the book, but she didn't want to give my copy away without my permission."

"So, did someone else come in and borrow it?" I asked.

"Yeah," Burt answered. "Local guy who was living in the campground because he was having problems at home. He came in with his rent and asked to borrow it. Said Alicia recommended it."

"Do you know his name?" I asked.

Burt scratched his head. "He paid his rent in cash. Give me a second. I can figure it out. He worked for one of the local construction companies… Some sort of foreman… Oh, right. His name was David Watkins."

"Is he still living here?" I asked.

"No, he and his wife made up a few months back. He's been gone for a while," Burt said.

"Do you know if he's still living in Coventry?" I asked.

"Lady, I don't know what people do after they leave here. Why? Do you think he had anything to do with Alicia's death? I can't see it. He was such a charming and sweet man. Never made sense that he was having such bad marital problems. Always figured the wife was a witch."

For a moment, I couldn't believe Burt was taking a stab at witches in front of me. Then I realized he had no idea what I was and was just using the term to demean David Watkins' wife.

I figured I had all of the information I was going to get out of Burt, so I left. When I got out to my car, I called Nora.

"Hey, Kinsley. What's going on? I didn't expect to hear from you again," Nora said. There was an edge to her tone. I knew the press hadn't left her alone since a body was found in her basement, and by the tone of her voice, it almost sounded like she blamed me for that. How, though? She'd asked me to come investigate the ghost that had attacked her.

168

"I'm sorry about how things have turned out," I said.

"Well, you couldn't have known," Nora said and followed it up with a huge sigh. "I suppose I'm the one that dragged you into all of this. Have you figured out the connection between the ghost that attacked me and Alicia?"

I hadn't because I hadn't really thought about it...

"No, but I mean, we may never figure that out. Ghosts are weird. It could have been Alicia manifesting herself as... as someone she knew or someone she saw in a movie. It could have been some random ghost who hung around your house and decided it didn't like the skeleton being in the basement. They don't like things that remind them of death," I said.

"You mean that ghost could still be here happily hanging around because we got rid of the skeleton?" Nora asked.

"Could be, but has she bothered you?" I asked.

"No," Nora admitted. "Everything has been completely fine since the skeleton was removed."

"I think that's the best outcome we could have hoped for," I said. "At least it wasn't a demon."

"You're right," Nora said. "So, how can I help you? Or did you just call to check on me?"

"Well, I did want to know how you were doing, but I called to find out the name of the construction company that built your house," I said.

"Oh, yeah, sure. It was Acclaim Homes," she said.

After a few more minutes of polite chat, Nora and I ended the call. At that point, I put my car in gear and headed off for the Acclaim Homes office over on the new side of Coventry.

The construction office was a bust. The woman working at the front desk was a complete professional and wouldn't tell me anything about David Watkins. She wouldn't even tell me if he was still working there. I got the whole speech about coming back with a warrant again. It was always so much easier when I found a gossip or someone who hated their job or boss.

As I was getting back into my car to go home, a man approached me. I'd planned on going home and watching a movie. Thorn and the FBI could handle Alicia's death. What was I doing anyway? For the first time that day, it occurred to me that I could be making other people sick. I'd let my parents keep Laney because I was still contagious, and yet I was running around town breathing on people. Ugh, I felt dumb.

I had that same dumb, self-depreciating feeling when the man walked up to me. "I've had strep throat," I said. "You probably shouldn't get too close."

"Oh," he said with an endearing, nervous chuckle. "I think I'll be okay. I do really want to talk to you if you have a moment."

"All right," I said. "What about?"

"I was just in the office dropping off some paperwork for my boss, and I heard you talking about him," the man said.

"David Watkins is your boss?" I asked.

"He is, but, um… can we walk across the street over there? I don't want him to see me talking to you. It's just that he makes me sort of nervous, and I don't want it to get back to him that you were in the office asking about him and then I was talking about you," the man said and looked around nervously. "My name's Bryan. The house, you can see, it's totally open. You can't get trapped in there or anything. I just want to make it look like I'm still working."

"All right," I said. "I'll walk over there with you, but I'm staying close to the street."

"I totally get it," Bryan said and started walking across to the house he'd pointed out. I followed along quickly. "I just wanted to know why you're here about David. I mean… let me explain. I've had problems with him too. Not just here at work either. I think he's been having an inappropriate friendship with my teenage daughter."

That made the hair on the back of my neck stand up. "Why do you think that? Have you seen them together?" I asked.

"I think so, but I can't prove it. I can't get her to tell me anything either. And sometimes, when I go into her room to tell her goodnight, it's like someone was just there. I know that sounds weird, but sometimes you can just tell someone was in a room?"

"I do know what you're talking about," I said.

"And a couple of times her window was still open just a bit," Bryan said. "I don't know what to do, but if you know something... maybe you can help. Do you think he had something to do with that skeleton?"

The hair on the back of my neck had settled down, but when Bryan asked that, it stood up again. That had been a huge leap, and when I looked around, I realized I'd followed Bryan into the house. We were standing in a spot where it was difficult to see the street.

That meant it was difficult to see us too...

I looked at Bryan again, and the mask of sweetness and earnest concern had slipped away. Staring back at me were the cold eyes of a predator.

"You're David," I said, and my voice was barely above a whisper. I should have screamed, but all the air seemed to be stuck in my stupid sore throat.

"And you're not as smart as you think you are," he said. "It's always so easy with you people. A smile and a sad story, and you completely forgot that you were going to stay close to the road. You wanted the details so badly that you walked right into this spot. You know that because of the houses on either side of this one, it's nearly impossible to see us from outside. You'd basically have to be in the front of the house to even know we're here."

"What do you want?" I asked as I began backing up the way I came.

"I don't want anything from you except for you to go away," David said. "On second thought, why don't you tell me why you're involved in this? How did you come to be wrapped up in it? I've heard the stories about you being there when they found her bones in my little hiding place. So, was it you? Are you the reason I would've gotten caught?"

"Would've?" I asked. "You are caught. I know who you are, and I guess we both know now that you did it."

"Ah, yes, but you're not going to be around to tell anyone," a sinister smile spread across David's face.

I knew then that we were done talking. I'd only managed to put a few feet between the two of us as I'd slowly inched away from him. So, when I turned to scream and run, he was on me like a cat pouncing.

As one of his hands covered my mouth and nose, the other wrapped around my throat. I tried to kick backward but missed him.

The pressure his hand put on the outside of my neck made my throat burn like fire. Tears filled my eyes and made it hard for me to see. Without magic and drained from strength because of my illness, I was done. I'd finally been too stupid to live.

And then David let go. As he fell to the floor, he nearly dragged me down with me.

"Come on," a voice said, and a man grabbed my hand.

He hoisted me from kneeling back to my feet and dragged me out of the house. I wiped the tears away from my eyes with my free hand and gasped for breath.

"Who are you?" I wheezed out as we stopped in the middle of the road.

Well, I stopped. I'd followed one man to my doom moments before, and I didn't care if this one had just rescued me. I wasn't going anywhere with anybody but my husband.

I pulled out my phone and called 911, but I couldn't speak above a breathy whisper. So, I shoved the phone into the man's hands.

While I stood there trying to breathe, he talked to the dispatcher and kept an eye on the house he'd just pulled me from moments before. Given the chaos, a few more construction workers appeared from the houses in progress around us.

So even when David, bleeding from the head, appeared from the house and began to stagger toward us, a group of men and women stood protectively around me. "It's over," the man who had my phone said as he handed it back to me.

David tried to make a run for it, but the small crowd who had been protecting me lunged at him and held him until Thorn and his deputies arrived. Right behind them was the FBI.

"Who are you?" I asked the man again.

"I'm Bryan," he said and stuck his hand out to me. "The actual Bryan, and I've had my suspicions about that creep for a while. When I saw you follow him into the house, I hurried over. Sorry I didn't get to you fast enough."

"Oh, you got to me plenty fast enough," I said. "Thank you."

Epilogue

So, David wasn't just a creepy dude who had a thing for teenage girls. He also got himself involved in the drug trade.

Hence the RV Alicia had been living in when she died. Alicia had escaped from her parents in a car she'd stolen from an old woman who'd recently been put in a nursing home.

No one had reported it stolen because no one realized it was missing. Alicia was living out of that car when David spotted her at a roadside diner on a trip back from south of the border.

A trip in an RV stuffed full of drugs and cash. But the drugs and cash were inside the panels of the RV, so unless you knew they were there, you wouldn't know they were there.

Anyway, David spotted Alicia at a roadside diner. She looked depressed and was anxiously pressing the waitress for a meal that cost less than five dollars. While the waitress kindly tried to help Alicia figure something out, David saw an opportunity.

She was just the kind of girl he liked. Young and easy to manipulate because of desperation.

Or so he thought. You see, David thought he could kill two birds with one stone. He could offer this young woman the RV to live in, so he'd have someone to watch it until the cartel wanted what was stuffed inside of it, and he'd have his next victim.

Little did he know that while Alicia would accept the RV and even drive it to the campground so he could avoid that risk, she was never going to be interested in any kind of relationship with him... even if he left his wife and moved into the campground to be closer to her.

Alicia was naïve. She genuinely thought that she and David were friends. She really believed that he'd wanted to help her, and she was so starved for genuine affection that she fell for his trap.

Until the day he tried to force himself on her, and she revealed that she just wasn't into men. At all. Ever. For any reason.

What David suffered was known as a narcissistic injury. He flew into a rage and, as anyone who has ever dealt with a narcissist knows, they are most dangerous when their egos are injured.

He killed her. David snuffed out Alicia's life because she rejected him, and he felt entitled to her.

And he confessed to all of it in front of Thorn and the FBI in exchange for a plea deal that took the death penalty off the table.

But there would be no trial, and David would spend the rest of his miserable life in prison. Bryan's daughter was safe.

I finally got some rest and recovered from the strep throat.

"I also got something else," I said. "I got my green eyes back."

The black streaks in my hair faded to a funky purple. I kinda liked it.

"You're different," Thorn said one night as we sat on the sofa watching a movie.

"Different how?" I asked.

"I don't know… lighter?" Thorn said.

"Are you saying I've lost weight?" I asked with a chuckle before elbowing him in the gut playfully.

"No, I mean like you're glowing. Well, maybe not glowing. It's just something about the way the light hits you is different. You remind me of you except when you first got here," he said. "Before the stress of everything you've taken on here weighed you down."

"I'll take that as a compliment then," I said.

"Speaking of lights, I think we should turn them off. This zombie clown movie you picked for our date night is a little dark. It's hard to see," Thorn said.

"No problem," I said and without thinking about it, I lifted my hand and snapped my fingers.

And the lights went out...

"Kinsley, you just turned the lights out with magic," Thorn said.

"I did," I said and sat up straight. "I did it."

"Is your magic coming back?" he asked.

"It might be," I said. "Oh, man, that would be amazing."

At that moment, Meri came trotting down the stairs. I was pretty sure it was Meri anyway. Same face, but he'd grown at least three inches since the last time I'd seen him.

"You're welcome," he said.

"For what are we thankful?" Thorn asked.

"Well, not like you guys noticed, but I've been up in the attic library studying my butt off, and I figured out what was wrong with magic. I fixed it."

"If you fixed what was wrong with magic, then how are you getting so much bigger?" I asked.

"Because what was wrong with magic was you," Meri said. "You decided to focus your energy on Laney and being a Mom. You're so freaking powerful that you somehow managed to shut it all down. So, since I'm your familiar, I figured out a way to protect you from yourself. Magic's coming back, and I undid the wish spell."

"For real?" I asked. "That's all it took."

"You might want to… I don't know… maybe study magic yourself a little more. Maybe just a smidge. I don't know. You could consider it," he said and sashayed out of the room.

"Whatever," I mumbled under my breath.

"Whatever," he called back from the kitchen. "Since I solved the whole magic thing, could I get some bacon?"

I started to get up, but Thorn patted me on the leg. "I'll go. You just watch your zombie clowns. It's not really my thing anyway."

"Thorn Wilson, are you scared of clowns?" I asked as he made his way out of the room.

"I don't want to talk about it," he said. "But if I never saw another clown in my life, it would be all right with me."

Thank you for reading!

Made in the USA
Monee, IL
13 May 2021